Jackie Womack

"I Feel Like a Prisoner!"

"Three weeks of work without a break," Ivory cried.

Matthew glanced over her with an arrogant intimacy that made her flush.

"A prisoner? Locked up? Totally in my power?" His cool blue gaze swept slowly across her face. "No, not yet, Ivory."

She started to move away but his hand on her arm prevented her. "You wouldn't dare!"

The devil gleamed at her from his blue eyes as he bent and touched his lips to hers.

Everything inside of her protested, but Ivory's body refused to resist. "Wouldn't I dare, Ivory? Wouldn't I?"

SUSAN STEVENS
has been writing since she was eight years old; and it is still her favorite occupation. She lives in Northern England with her husband who, she says, is her greatest fan. She loves to travel and hopes to visit the United States soon!

Dear Reader:

Silhouette has always tried to give you exactly what you want. When you asked for increased realism, deeper characterization and greater length, we brought you Silhouette Special Editions. When you asked for increased sensuality, we brought you Silhouette Desire. Now you ask for books with the length and depth of Special Editions, the sensuality of Desire, but with something else besides, something that no one else offers. Now we bring you SILHOUETTE INTIMATE MOMENTS, true romance novels, longer than the usual, with all the depth that length requires. More sensuous than the usual, with characters whose maturity matches that sensuality. Books with the ingredient no one else has tapped: excitement.

There is an electricity between two people in love that makes everything they do magic, larger than life—and this is what we bring you in SILHOUETTE INTIMATE MOMENTS. Look for them wherever you buy books.

These books are for the woman who wants more than she has ever had before. These books are for you. As always, we look forward to your comments and suggestions. You can write to me at the address below:

Karen Solem
Editor-in-Chief
Silhouette Books
P.O. Box 769
New York, N.Y. 10019

SUSAN STEVENS
Ivory Innocence

Silhouette Romance

Published by Silhouette Books New York

America's Publisher of Contemporary Romance

SILHOUETTE BOOKS, a Simon & Schuster Division of
GULF & WESTERN CORPORATION
1230 Avenue of the Americas, New York, N.Y. 10020

Copyright © 1983 by Susan Stevens

Distributed by Pocket Books

ISBN: 0-671-57230-X

First Silhouette Books printing June, 1983

10 9 8 7 6 5 4 3 2 1

Map by Ray Lundgren

America's Publisher of Contemporary Romance

Printed in the U.S.A.

Ivory
Innocence

Chapter One

"Your mother was a Meldrum, Ivory. That makes you a Meldrum, too. Never forget it."

The words her grandmother had repeated so often rang like a litany in her head as she left the main road and turned off among the rolling hills of South Lincolnshire. It was a place of sturdy farmhouses, of fields hugging the contours of the undulating land in swathes of tender green and bright yellow, with yarrow making drifts of white under the roadside hedges.

Driving up a familiar rise, Ivory braked as she came in sight of the village of Hedley Magna. It lay in a hollow, its houses built mainly of pale limestone interspersed with newer brick dwellings. The red of the pantiled roofs, mellowed over the years, contrasted softly with the greens of the late spring landscape.

Just beyond the brow of the hill, a line of chestnut trees with their erect candle blossoms sheltered a sign that read TOP FARM. Ivory turned in beneath the trees, driving along a rutted lane between meadows where cows grazed, past barns and outbuildings to a yard where the farmhouses stood to one side.

As Ivory stopped the car, a fair-haired young man wearing muddied overalls and Wellington boots emerged from the old stable block and came clumping over, greeting her with a smile.

"So you got here, then."

Tired from driving and tense because of what she had come to do, she bit back a sarcastic retort and instead forced a smile.

"Hello, Rob. Yes, I made it. It took me longer than I expected, though. Would you mind taking my overnight case for me? I really mustn't stop or I'll be late for my appointment. I'm due at the Hall at three o'clock."

She took her small case from the backseat and handed it to Rob Garth, nervously touching her silvergold hair, arranged in a chignon.

"How do I look?"

He considered her carefully, his hazel eyes warm with affection as he took in the neat gray suit with its flared skirt lying smoothly across slim hips, and the little jacket that fitted closely to her curves. Beneath it she wore a navy blouse, with a floppy bow tied at her throat.

"Wonderful!" he declared.

Ivory sighed. "No, really, Rob. Do I look efficient and capable? Like a teacher?"

"I suppose so. But when I was at school I never had a teacher who looked like you. I might have concentrated harder if I had."

In no mood for flattery, Ivory opened the car door and slid back behind the wheel. "I want Matthew Kendrake to employ me, not seduce me," she said tartly; then, seeing the hurt in his eyes, "I'm sorry, Rob. I'm all on edge. Talk to you later."

Aware that he stood watching her with the air of a puppy that had been slapped for something he hadn't done, she turned the car around, and drove back up the lane to the road. The chestnuts hid her from the farmhouse as she let the car ease down the lane toward the village, and she pulled up in a shady spot where trees hung over a wrought-iron fence and small gate. Beyond it she could see the golden walls of Hedley Hall. But her attention was on the building opposite— the cottage that had once been her home.

Her gray eyes grew bleak as she stared at the scaffolding that surrounded the place. New windows had been cut, but the blackened marks of fire remained smudged across the light stone and the roof was a maze of joists where once there had been thatch. The weeds grew tall in the garden her grandparents had tended so lovingly.

After a year haunted by nightmares of fire, the memories still brought pain that choked her throat with tears. She silently renewed her vow to find out the truth and repay the Kendrakes for what they had done.

She put the car into gear again and drove on down the curving lane to where, at a junction with another road, she came face to face with the church. Here on the corner she came to the main driveway of Hedley Hall. The big house hid behind woods of beech, lime and field maple, and among the thick undergrowth ground ivy crept round patches of bluebells and forget-me-nots.

The gravel drive curved around through the trees until the house came into sight behind sweeps of lawn. It was built of Lincolnshire limestone that glowed golden in the sunlight, and its formal Georgian lines, with tall windows and balustraded roof, were softened by drapes of clematis leaves.

Pulling up on the broad graveled area that fronted the house, Ivory left the car and smoothed back her hair. The style left the lines of her face uncluttered: wide-spaced gray eyes fringed with dark lashes, high cheekbones and generous mouth.

At the moment that mouth was set in stubborn lines, and her eyes glinted like steel as she surveyed the waiting house. For generations the Hall had belonged to the Meldrum family—her family—until a Kendrake had robbed her grandfather of his heritage. As the last of the Meldrums, she was embarking on a quest to avenge the wrong that had been done long before she was born.

With her navy handbag swinging from her shoulder, she crunched across the gravel to the wide stone porch, where a wooden tub of flowers stood beside a doormat. She pressed the bell and heard faint chimes sound somewhere in the depths of the house.

After a few moments the door was opened by a middle-aged woman in a dark dress. She regarded Ivory inquiringly.

"My name is Andersen," Ivory said. "I have an appointment with Mr. Kendrake."

"Oh, yes, Miss Andersen." The woman smiled, stepping back to open the door wider. "He's expecting you. Please come in."

Ivory walked into the hall, glancing around at its spacious proportions. It was furnished with quiet good taste; framed watercolors graced the walls, and a line of oval miniatures followed the curve of the stairs. Somehow, it wasn't quite what Ivory had been expecting.

"I'm Mrs. Barnes, the housekeeper," the woman said with a smile. "If you'll come this way, I believe Mr. Kendrake's waiting for you. He'll be pleased you're on time. He doesn't like to be kept waiting."

She led the way down the hall and threw open a door to announce, "Miss Andersen is here, sir."

"Show her in," a deep male voice replied, and Mrs. Barnes turned to give Ivory another encouraging smile.

Head held high, she stepped into what turned out to be a sitting room, furnished in gold and blue with much rich brocade and gleaming mahogany. Sunlight streamed in, darkening the tall figure who stood by the open French windows. Beyond him, Ivory glimpsed a terrace and a stretch of daisy-starred lawn; then the man turned, drawing her full attention.

Although her face showed only polite interest, she was startled by her first sight of Matthew Kendrake. He looked to be in his mid-thirties, a lean, rangy man wearing tailored slacks and a thin woolen sweater. As he walked toward her, away from the bright sunlight, she saw a deeply tanned face with hard contours, topped by dark hair that seemed windblown into tousled waves. But it was his eyes that most surprised her, eyes of an amazing forget-me-not blue—like the flowers that grew in his woods.

No, not *his* woods, Ivory amended the thought: *Meldrum* woods. By rights this whole estate was Meldrum property. But she kept her expression noncommittal and her eyes steady on the dark-faced man.

He paused a few feet away to look her over from head to foot, then said, "You're younger than I expected."

"I'm almost twenty-two," Ivory replied levelly. "In your letter, you didn't specify any age."

"No, I suppose I didn't," he said, a crease forming between his dark brows. "I don't suppose it matters, if your qualifications are as good as you claim."

Opening her handbag, Ivory drew out the large envelope that contained her certificates and letters of recommendation from college. She had no doubt they were impressive; she had been a good student and gained high marks in her final exams less than a year before, despite the fact that she had been numb with grief.

Matthew Kendrake took the envelope, gesturing her into a chair. "Have a seat, Miss Andersen."

"Thank you." She sank down among brocade cushions, coolly surveying the bent head of the man who was her adversary. He sat opposite her, perusing her documents as if trying to find some flaw, and Ivory wondered what he would do if he guessed her purpose. She viewed him with detachment. Broad shoulders filled out the sweater that was the same bright blue as his eyes; long legs sprawled across the deep carpet, clad in slacks with knife-sharp creases; and his hair was so dark brown as to be almost black, curling untidily round his ears and down his neck.

She almost flinched when he suddenly lifted his head and fixed her with his forget-me-not eyes.

"These are very good," he said. His voice was a deep drawl, and Ivory wondered where he came from. Not that it made any difference. By the time she had finished with him, he would gladly slink off back to the place that had been his home before.

"Thank you," she replied, lowering her eyes so that her thoughts wouldn't show.

"But you still haven't been able to find a job?" he asked.

Sighing, she allowed her candid gaze to meet his again. "I'm afraid not. Things are very difficult for teachers at the moment. I've been filling in by working for some friends who own a restaurant, though that hasn't stopped me from applying for teaching posts."

"Which is why you want to tutor my daughter," he said.

"I'd rather use my training than do other work," Ivory replied. Her grandmother had struggled to allow her to attend college and to waste those years seemed a betrayal. The fact that this particular job meant living at Hedley Hall was a bonus she had not planned for.

"I'm intrigued to know how you found out I needed a tutor for Janey," Matthew Kendrake said, lounging back in his chair.

Ivory sat primly, her knees together and hands folded in her lap, her severe hairstyle and sensible clothes making her the picture of the perfect teacher—formal, correct, and just a little old-fashioned. It was an image she had chosen carefully.

"I have friends in the village," she explained. "They happened to mention that they had heard you were thinking of hiring a teacher for your daughter."

"And how did your friends find out?" Matthew Kendrake asked. "I haven't yet got round to advertising the post. All I've done is talk about it, in the privacy of my own home."

"Village grapevines are notorious, aren't they?" Ivory said demurely. "But you do realize we should have to ask the permission of the Local Education Authority? If a child has to be educated at home, they usually supply a teacher."

"So I'd heard. But I want a little more than just a teacher who would come in for a few hours each day. My daughter needs a companion, too. She's not a strong child. Recently she has spent some months in the hospital; before that she missed a good deal of schooling for one reason and another, but the doctors tell me she's ready to take up school again. Unfortunately, my business interests take me away frequently, but it would be unfair to ask Mrs. Barnes to have charge of Janey on any permanent basis. If I can organize it with the Local Authority, I assume there'd be no problem from your point of view about coming to live here?"

"No, none at all."

"No family objections? Since I'm a widower, your parents may have their doubts about your staying here."

"I have no family," Ivory said. "Besides, Mr. Kendrake, if you're worried about gossip, your housekeeper will provide a perfect chaperon to preserve both our reputations."

A glint of amusement hovered in his eyes. Ivory was aware that she was not quite what he had had in mind when he planned to employ a tutor-companion. Most probably he had visualized someone older, someone plump and homely to play nanny to his daughter. But at least he had not dismissed her as a candidate at first sight.

"This would be a full-time job," he said. "More than nine to five, five days a week."

"I'm prepared for that," Ivory said evenly. "Since I have no commitments elsewhere, it won't be a hardship for me."

While they discussed salary—which was generous—and the further details of her employment, she could not help but notice the way Matthew Kendrake's blue glance kept roaming across her face and figure. Despite himself, it seemed, he found her attractive. But she was careful not to respond to the flattering perusal and rationed her smiles, keeping her voice impersonal.

Eventually, he unfolded his long body from the chair and said, "Before we go any further, you'd better meet my daughter. Her opinion is as important as mine, since she's the one who will be spending all her time with you."

"Yes, of course." Ivory gracefully got to her feet, and Matthew Kendrake took another sidelong look at the neat jacket that hugged her figure, his glance going down to trim calves and ankles set off by high heels.

"This way," he said, and led her out through the French windows, onto the terrace.

Ivy twined shiny dark leaves around the balustrade and edged the steps that led down to the lawn where pink-tipped daisies grew in profusion. As they walked up a slight rise, the hollow in front of them opened out, and Ivory was surprised to see a kidney-shaped swimming pool nestling behind a bank of shrubs. A path led down to the pool, and on the grass to one side a playhouse stood beneath a shimmering lime tree. There a small girl sat talking earnestly to a row of dolls.

Matthew Kendrake had said that his daughter was eight, but she was small for her age, very thin, with a mop of brown curls.

"Janey?" he called as they approached.

The child looked round and got awkwardly to her feet, huge brown eyes almost eclipsing her face as she stared at Ivory.

"This is Miss Andersen," Matthew Kendrake said.

The little girl held out a hand and said faintly, "How do you do?"

Even in that first moment, something about Janey touched Ivory's heart. The child looked lost, sad, and extremely vulnerable, appealing to a maternal instinct that Ivory had not guessed was in her. Of course she liked children, but she had never met one who made her feel so instantly protective.

"Miss Andersen may be coming to look after you," Matthew Kendrake said, laying a hand on his daughter's shoulder. Ivory saw how the child flinched and then steeled herself to accept her father's touch, but all the time her liquid brown eyes were fixed on Ivory's face.

"What are you doing with the dolls, Janey?" she asked.

"Playing school," came the wary reply.

"That's good," her father said, much too heartily. "Do you think you'd like having Miss Andersen help you catch up on some of the things you've missed?" He towered over the unhappy child. "She hasn't been very well lately," he added. "But she's much better now and raring to go. Aren't you, Janey?"

"Yes," the child said.

Ivory heard the irritable sigh that escaped him. Clearly he was annoyed with his own daughter, who seemed inhibited by his presence. He was too patronizing and heavy-handed, Ivory thought. No wonder Janey seemed half afraid of him.

"Do you think Janey and I could have a few minutes together to get acquainted?" she asked.

He lifted a questioning eyebrow, but there was relief in the brilliant blue eyes. "Good idea. Yes, do that. I'll ask Mrs. Barnes to make some tea. Come in when you're ready."

Ivory watched as he strode away with athletic movements, the close-fitting slacks hugging the contours of slim hips and muscular thighs. He was, she thought, a man who would be more at home among other men than with his own motherless child, who stood obediently waiting for Ivory to make the next move.

Smiling at the child, Ivory sat down on the grass, looking at the scribbles on a pink notepad. "What's the lesson today? Ah, sums. Are they any good at sums?"

"They're only dolls," Janey said scornfully. "They're not really doing sums."

"Well, I know that, but it's fun to pretend, don't you think? I used to play hospital and have all my dolls in bed. Do you do that?"

Janey sank cross-legged on the lawn, conceding, "Sometimes. I was in hospital. It was good fun—

especially when I started to get better. There were a lot of other children to play with."

"I'm sure you'll make friends in the village before long," Ivory said softly.

"I would, if Daddy would let me go out," the child replied, sighing as she sprawled on the daisy-strewn grass.

There was very little wrong with her mind, Ivory decided, but if she had been ill that would explain her physical frailty. All she really needed was for someone to take a real interest in her. She had lost her mother, and her father was often away, he had said. From what Ivory had seen of the relationship, the father was ill at ease with the child, and Janey appeared nervous of him.

"If you come to live with us," Janey said suddenly, looking with earnest dark eyes into Ivory's face, "does that mean I won't have to go to boarding school?"

"Boarding school?" Ivory echoed.

"That's what Carla wants to do with me," the child said bitterly. "I heard her saying to Daddy that boarding school would be the answer."

"As far as I know, he's intending to keep you here," Ivory assured her.

But Janey was not convinced. "Is that what he said? What did he say your name was?"

"Miss Andersen. But why not call me Ivory? It's much easier. And if I do come, I want us to be friends, Janey."

"I'd like that too," Janey said. "At least you're not like Carla. Carla's rotten!"

Ivory was surprised to see hatred twist the child's wan face. "Who's Carla?"

"She's Daddy's friend." Suddenly she confronted Ivory with burning brown eyes. "I hate her!"

"But I'm sure your father wouldn't send you away if you don't want to go," Ivory replied, worried by the violent emotions that ran through the child.

"He would if Carla wanted him to," Janey said flatly. "I know he would!"

Leaping up, she dodged into the playhouse and closed the flap as if wanting to be alone.

Deciding not to press matters at that point, Ivory stood up. Brushing down her skirt, she said quietly, "I'm going in now, Janey. Will you come?"

There was no answer. Janey had retreated into her hurt little shell, and to probe now would only make her shut herself away further.

"Well, come and say good-bye to me before I go," Ivory called. "I'm going to have that cup of tea."

As she walked back over the lawn, her mind was on the unhappy child. She felt she could help Janey, if she was allowed a chance, though she had not expected to feel so involved so quickly.

Lifting a hand to smooth a blowing tendril of spun-gold hair, she paused on the edge of the terrace as she saw Matthew Kendrake lounging in the doorway watching her. His face expressed nothing, but she knew he had been standing there for some seconds, watching her approach.

"I was about to call you," he said. "Mrs. Barnes has brought the tea."

"Oh, thank you."

His glance swept her again, lingering near her hip. "You've got grass stains on your skirt."

"Oh, no!" She looked at the offending green smears, brushed ineffectually at them, and sighed. "I expect they'll come off."

"Yes, probably."

Alerted by a strange tautness in his voice, Ivory

lifted her eyes to him, but found his face expressionless, bland. "Come inside and sit down."

Since he didn't move, she was obliged to pass close to him, his proximity making her aware of the power in his muscled body. He strolled after her and resumed his own chair, and leaned to pour tea from a silver pot into delicate china cups.

"And how did you get along with my daughter?" he inquired as he passed her a full cup. "She's a peculiar little thing, don't you think?"

Ivory's eyebrows knotted at the description so negligently expressed. She sipped the hot tea, feeling it ease her dry throat before she dared raise her eyes. When she did, she was in control of herself.

"I don't think any child is 'peculiar,' Mr. Kendrake," she said levelly. "They have their little quirks like the rest of us. Janey seems to be a trifle insecure, but that's hardly surprising."

"Oh?" His eyebrow slanted questioningly. "Why not?"

"I understand you haven't been in Hedley Magna very long," she replied, returning his look with cool gray eyes. "Children often find a move unsettling. And Janey has no mother. May I ask how long it is since your wife—"

"Six months," he said flatly.

"I see. Then that's another factor, another blow for Janey."

She was amazed when his mouth twisted into a cynical smile. "You think so?"

"Of course it was! Have you been so busy with your own grief that—" Embarrassed, she stopped herself and looked down at her tea. "Forgive me, I had no right to say that. But Janey is obviously unhappy. If I'm to take care of her, she must be my main concern."

"Really?" Irony was strong in his voice. "Even if you have to fight with me to protect her?"

Very slowly, Ivory lifted her head until her eyes met the mocking blue ones. "I would hope we could cooperate, but . . . Yes, Mr. Kendrake, if you employ me I shall, if necessary, fight you for what I believe is right for Janey."

His gaze swept her with open amusement, telling her he found little to fear in her slender femininity. "I shall certainly be careful not to underestimate you, Miss Andersen. Let us hope we can see eye to eye over Janey's welfare." Pausing, he rubbed a long finger down his nose. "She has obviously made a great impression on you."

"Yes, she has," Ivory agreed.

"And you on her? Though not enough to persuade her to brave my presence, I notice." He smiled wryly at Ivory's look of surprise. "I'm quite aware that as far as Janey is concerned I'm an ogre. If you can help us achieve a closer understanding, I'll be grateful."

"I shall do my best," Ivory said. "Do I gather you're offering me the job?"

"Let's make it a three-months' trial, shall we?" he suggested. "I'll contact the Education people tomorrow and arrange it. How soon can you start?"

"I could move up here next weekend, if that's convenient."

"Fine. Now have your tea before it gets too cold. I'll go and bring Janey in to hear the good news."

Ivory watched him walk out to the terrace, a frown on her face. He was an enigmatic man. She suspected that he found having a small daughter more of a drawback than a blessing.

Hearing him roar, "Janey! Janey, come back here!" at the top of his voice, Ivory put down her empty cup and went out, to see Janey fleeing as if from the devil himself, coming toward the house with her father storming angrily behind her. She darted up the steps, flung herself past Ivory, and rushed through the sitting room and into the hall, slamming the door behind her.

Bewildered, Ivory stared after the child, then heard Matthew Kendrake behind her breathing hard in his fury.

"What happened?" she asked. When there was no reply, she whirled round to look into snapping blue eyes above lips compressed so tightly they were rimmed with white. "Mr. Kendrake! If she's been ill you really ought to—"

"I won't have her swearing at me!" he said through his teeth.

"Swearing? Surely she didn't—"

"I assure you, she did! She's been allowed to get away with too much because she's been ill. I shall expect you to teach her to curb her temper, Miss Andersen. I won't be spoken to like that."

"But what caused it?" Ivory asked.

"She refused to come out of that playhouse when I told her to. Something put her into one of her stubborn moods. Was it you?"

Inwardly flinching under the rage that simmered behind his eyes, Ivory straightened her back. "She was upset when I left her, but not because of anything I'd said or done."

"Then why?" he demanded.

"She—she said something about being afraid you might send her away to boarding school."

A sharp laugh escaped him. "I would have thought the prospect of leaving me behind might appeal to her. Boarding school? What put that into her head?"

"Apparently she overheard you discussing it with someone."

"I see." He thrust his hands into his pockets, his jaw

thrust out aggressively. "So Mrs. Barnes isn't the only member of my household who's given to eavesdropping. Well, I sincerely hope you'll cure my daughter of any such tendencies, Miss Andersen. And I can assure you, I have no intention of sending her anywhere. Obviously, she's already spent far too much time away from my influence. I take my responsibilities seriously. I hope you do, too."

"Yes, I do," Ivory said stoutly. How he could call little Janey a "responsibility" in that grim way was a mystery to her.

The more she saw of Matthew Kendrake, the more she was convinced that he was an exact replica of his uncle: George Kendrake, the man who had ruined her grandfather. They were both cold, calculating, and utterly ruthless.

Chapter Two

Feeling some need for reassurance, Ivory left her car in the lane and walked across to the church, through the wooden gate and along the path between the yews. Inside, on stones carved with names and dates, the church walls bore evidence of her Meldrum ancestors, who had once been masters of Hedley Hall. Ivory renewed her acquaintance with them all, recalling how her grandmother had pointed the memorials out to her when she was a child no older than Janey Kendrake. Mrs. Meldrum had been proud of her heritage and had taught Ivory to be proud, too.

The cottage on the hill was the only real home Ivory could remember. She recalled nothing of her early life in Africa, where she had been born.

"Why your mother had to marry Nils Andersen I shall never know," her grandmother had been wont to say with a sigh. "Of course he was tough and good-looking—brown as a berry and fair as Apollo—but then who wouldn't be, living in the sun the way he did? He was a typical wild Colonial, but there was nothing we could do to stop your mother from marrying him and going out to that farm in Kenya."

Ivory had been born on the farm. But shortly before her fourth birthday her parents had been killed when a duststorm brought down their plane as they flew back from a business trip to Nairobi. Their small daughter was hastily brought home to England, to live with her grandparents in the cottage at Hedley Magna.

Her early life had been uneventful. Her grandmother seemed able to perform miracles on a tight budget. There were riding lessons, piano lessons, and the excitement of a brand-new bicycle when Ivory was eleven years old.

"You need these things," her grandmother had often said. "You're a Meldrum. I can't let our neighbors think the Meldrums are living on the breadline. That wouldn't be proper."

The fact that she was a Meldrum had been drummed into Ivory from an early age, and over the years she learned what lay behind this schooling: when her grandfather had been a young man, he had inherited Hedley Hall and its estate, which included the vast acreage of Home Farm and half the village properties. But he had been cheated out of his lands by a man named George Kendrake.

"All because of jealousy," Mrs. Meldrum declared. "George Kendrake courted me—he was one of many, I may tell you. I was quite a beauty in my day. But when I married your grandfather, George Kendrake was so bitterly jealous that he set out to ruin us."

The story was told so often that Ivory learned it by heart, but she listened patiently every time her grandmother was in the mood to reminisce. It was always her grandmother who spoke in anger about George Kendrake; her grandfather said only, "That's all in the past."

Ivory grew to detest the sight of the tall, ramrod-straight figure of George Kendrake, whom she saw occasionally when he came to spend a weekend at the Hall with friends.

"Just look at him!" her grandmother would say in disgust. "Playing lord of the manor. He pretended to be our friend, but all the time he was plotting, using your grandfather's trusting nature to ruin him and take the Hall. All he left us was this cottage."

Ivory had never clearly understood the nature of the swindle; Mrs. Meldrum spoke vaguely of bad financial advice given by George Kendrake, and business deals that went wrong. What was not in doubt was the fact that in time, through the influence of his "friend," John Meldrum faced bankruptcy.

"That was when George Kendrake played his ace," Mrs. Meldrum had said. "He stepped in and offered to buy the estate, which was what he'd been scheming for all along. If it hadn't been for that man, we'd still be living at Hedley Hall."

Ivory remembered her grandfather as a gentle man who had grown sadder as he grew older, a bent, graying figure pottering aimlessly about while his wife valiantly attempted to keep up appearances.

Mrs. Meldrum had chaired the local Women's Institute and been on the flower roster at the church. She gave coffee mornings for good causes and helped out at jumble sales, as if she were still the lady of the manor. Most people respected her for it; most of the local people regarded George Kendrake with contempt. Ivory sometimes wondered if that was why he had chosen not to live at the Hall but had used it as a weekend retreat.

Ivory was at college when her grandfather died suddenly. She returned to Hedley Magna to find her grandmother distraught and showing her age. Ivory did her best to offer comfort, but the old lady refused to be consoled.

"When I've passed my finals," Ivory promised, "I'll come home and find a job somewhere near. I won't leave you alone. There's one consolation, grandmother: you've still got the cottage."

Mrs. Meldrum had raised drowned, red-rimmed eyes and sobbed, "Oh, Ivory, if you only knew! If you only knew!"

But she wouldn't say what it was that Ivory didn't know, and Ivory was left to guess that something other than her husband's death was distressing her.

Fate had its ironic laugh when, only a few months later, the perfidious George Kendrake died. Mrs. Meldrum wrote and informed Ivory of the news with great bitterness:

> I can't feel sorry. I shall always hate that man. I'd have thought more kindly of him if he'd just stabbed your grandfather, but instead he killed him slowly, over forty years. And I hear he's left the estate to his nephew—another Kendrake to put his curse on the village. I expect he, too, will be an absentee landlord, since to my knowledge he's never been near the place. He lives abroad somewhere, so they say.
>
> Ivory, it's so unfair. The Hall should be yours instead of going to some stranger who cares nothing for it. But I shall make sure he receives a cool welcome when he comes to claim his ill-gotten inheritance.

Unfortunately, months before Matthew Kendrake arrived, Mrs. Meldrum died, in a fire that gutted the cottage just before Easter in Ivory's last year at college. Even now, over a year later, Ivory vividly recalled how she had stood in pouring rain and stared in disbelief at the burned-out shell of the place that had been her home for sixteen years. Investigators said an electrical fault was to blame, but in Ivory's shocked mind this tragedy, too, could be laid at the Kendrakes' door. Everything she loved had, literally, gone up in smoke.

Grieving, she had visited the solicitor and heard even more shocking news: the cottage had not belonged to her grandparents; it was still part of the Hall estate.

Ivory recalled sitting in the solicitor's office and reading the letter her grandmother had left for her:

I'm afraid it's the truth, Ivory. I always believed we owned the cottage, until your grandfather died, when I found out that he had been paying rent to George Kendrake. He must have kept it from me to save me from knowing that we were virtually living on that man's charity. And I have done the same for your sake. But now I must write the truth. George Kendrake took everything. There's nothing of value I can leave for you, except my bits and pieces of jewelry. But at least I know you will have the capital that came from the sale of your father's farm in Kenya. I hope you understand why I had to use the interest, on your behalf, to keep you and give you those little extras, and to put you through college. Oh, my dear, life has been cruel for us all, but I did my best for you. God bless and keep you, my love, and never forget—you're a Meldrum.

Ivory had been surprised by the amount of the legacy she was due to inherit on her twenty-first birthday, but the money had meant little to her. She went back to college to take her final exams and then went to stay with friends in Bournemouth, on the south coast, far away from memories. She had believed she could never bear to come back to Hedley Magna, but as her grief passed she began to form a plan. Her legacy might be enough to buy the Hall if she could find proof of George Kendrake's treachery and persuade his nephew to sell the estate back to her—if necessary under the threat of revealing his uncle as a heartless villain.

She did not like the idea of blackmail, but as a last resort she had promised herself to use it.

But before she had a chance to do anything more, Rob Garth, her childhood friend from Hedley Magna, had written one of his long chatty letters, which included the news that Matthew Kendrake had taken residence in the Hall and was thinking of employing a teacher to help his little daughter. It was the opening Ivory had been needing. She would come back to Hedley Magna and spy out the land before making any further moves.

Her one regret had been that George Kendrake himself was no longer alive to regret his perfidy toward her grandparents. But now that she had met his nephew, she knew him to be exactly the same sort of man as his uncle. There must be something about Kendrake blood that turned their men into monsters. Ivory was prepared to use any weapon she could think of to settle old scores.

As she left the church, a bus drew up by the junction and discharged a few schoolchildren. A young girl with golden hair fastened into pigtails over her ears called good-bye to her friends and set off up the lane, her bag trailing from one hand.

"Becky!" Ivory called, hurrying across the road.

Rebecca Garth turned, her face puckered in a frown,

then her smile beamed. "Oh, hello, Ivory! I'd forgotten you were coming today."

"Let me give you a lift," Ivory said, indicating the car that waited beneath swaying branches of sticky lime leaves. "I'm on my way back to the farm now."

"Oh, great!" Rebecca said. "I'm worn out. We've been playing rounders the last two lessons. I was bowler. I'm good at that. I can throw really hard. Is this your car? I didn't know you could drive. Is it true you're coming to work at the Hall? What's the new girl like? I've never seen her. Mrs. Barnes told Mum she's delicate."

"I gather she's been ill," Ivory said. "But I'm sure she would be pleased to make a friend."

As they climbed into the car, Ivory remembered that Rob's little sister had always been a happy little chatterer. She was the darling of the family, having come so late after her brother. She had been little more than a baby when her father had died and Rob had taken over responsibility for running the farm.

"Did you see they're doing your old cottage up?" Rebecca asked as they passed the scaffolded building. "It's been funny, having it stand empty. Martin Ward said it was haunted, but I've never seen anything, though it was creepy going past in the dark last winter."

She kept up the flow of conversation as the car moved up the hill and turned beneath the chestnuts to the farm, where Ivory parked in the yard close to the house. From the barn came the sound of voices, clatterings and bangs, and the swish of a hose as someone rinsed down the floor.

Mrs. Garth appeared at the back door, wiping her hands on a flowered apron. A petite, wiry woman with straight brown hair, she had a ruddy face that lit with a smile as she held out her arms to greet Ivory and accept a kiss on the cheek.

"You look well, dear," she remarked. "It's lovely to see you again. Now, Becky, we're going to have some tea, so don't go rushing out to the pony just yet. Come and sit down, Ivory. Rob'll be in soon. I've made some sandwiches and scones, and we'll have a hot supper later. Does that suit you?"

"I'll fit in with whatever you've planned," Ivory said, taking off her jacket before sitting at one of the chairs by the big table. "It was very kind of you to offer to put me up for the night," Ivory said, feeling at home in the familiar room. "I wouldn't have fancied having to drive all the way back to Bournemouth this evening."

"I should just think not!" said Mrs. Garth. "Why, you look tired out. How did you get on—or shouldn't I ask?"

"Very well, thank you. Mr. Kendrake offered me the job, on a three-months' trial basis. I'll be coming back next Saturday to make a start."

"So soon?"

"There didn't seem to be any point in delaying. Janey seems a bit difficult at the moment, and Mrs. Barnes has enough on her hands, looking after that huge house."

She looked around as she heard Rob come in the door. He grinned at her. "So you'll be coming back to Hedley after all. That'll be nice, won't it, Mum?"

"Lovely," his mother agreed. "We've missed you, Ivory. We missed you when you were away at college, but at least you came home for holidays. This year it's seemed strange, with the cottage standing there."

"I know," Ivory said softly.

After tea, she went out to look at the pony grazing in the field behind the orchard with two other horses. Cherry, as Rebecca called him, was entirely black except for a few white hairs in his tail. He came trotting to the fence and nuzzled Rebecca's hand while Ivory stroked his head.

"Why Cherry?" Ivory asked.

"Well, you have black cherries, don't you?" Rebecca said with unassailable logic. Tossing her golden hair, she scrambled over the fence and leapt up to the pony's back, grabbing the rope bridle. She urged him into a trot, showing off for Ivory's benefit.

"A little brat, isn't she?" Rob said fondly, coming to lean on the fence beside Ivory. "She reminds me of you, not many years ago."

"Oh, thanks," Ivory said drily.

"I was wondering," Rob added. "Would you like to go out for a drink after supper? I've got some chores to do first, but if we go about nine we'll have time for a couple of beers. Okay?"

"Yes, fine," Ivory said.

Smiling, Rob touched her arm and sauntered away, the sun gilding his tousled fair hair as he ducked under apple tree branches. A shower of fading blossoms fluttered onto the grass, their pink glory almost gone now that the leaves were unfurling.

After supper she drove with Rob down to the pub, with its low black beams hung with hunting prints and a huge fireplace where a brass urn full of flowers stood. Several people recognized her and asked how she was doing. It was some time before she was able to escape to a corner table alone with Rob.

"The village hasn't seemed the same since your grandmother died," he told her. "She was an institution—the last old-fashioned lady of the manor, even if she had fallen on hard times."

"She was a proud woman," Ivory said.

"Brave, too. I've often wondered why they stayed in Hedley."

"They belonged here!" she said passionately. "But their very presence must have been a reminder to George Kendrake of what he'd done. Why do you think he stayed away from the Hall? His conscience must have troubled him. Unfortunately, it didn't trouble him enough, or he'd have tried to make amends. It makes me so angry when I think—"

Rob's hand covered hers, stopping the flow of bitterness. "Hush, love. It's no good getting agitated about it. It's all ancient history. And you're going to have to work at the Hall."

"Yes." Still trembling with rage, she pulled her hand free of his clasp, making Rob give her a puzzled sidelong look.

"I can't really understand why you want to go there, Ivory," he said. "I hope you're not going to regret it. It won't be easy, being an employee and knowing all the time that your ancestors lived there in style."

Ivory sipped her lager and lime, her eyes on the round table in front of her. Not for anything would she have Rob guess her real reason for applying for the post of tutor to Janey Kendrake.

"I just want to work at the job I'm trained for," she said. "I'm wasting my time in Bournemouth, working in the restaurant and staying with Merry and Bill. They've been very kind, but I know they'd prefer their privacy, and there are plenty of people who will be only too happy to do waitressing work for them. Since I can't get a job in a school, I may as well work for Matthew Kendrake. Little Janey needs someone. It's obvious her father is hopeless with her. He seems to regard her as a liability, and she knows it."

A stir among the crowd by the bar drew her attention to the man who had just come in, as if by mentioning his name she had summoned him from the elements. Matthew Kendrake, with a sports jacket over his blue sweater, strode to the bar. The crowd parted for him. The hum of conversation dwindled, and more than one man deliberately turned his back on the newcomer. The hostility grew so thick that Ivory wondered why the air didn't creak with it.

She drew back into the shadows behind the side wing of the bench, hoping that Matthew Kendrake would not see her. She heard him order a bottle of scotch, taking a wallet from his hip pocket. He appeared not to notice the wary looks of the villagers but stood relaxed, his tailored slacks clinging to muscular calves.

Despite herself, Ivory stared at his lean, tall figure, the thick, wavy dark hair bathed in pink light from a lamp above the bar; the broad shoulders, the elegant hang of his jacket. She had never seen a man quite so well made, with such lithe power evident in his every move. Dangerous, she thought again. Dangerously attractive, if she was honest.

He spoke pleasantly to the landlord, thanking him and remarking on the fine weather, then he said good night and walked out as if oblivious to the tension he had created. As the door swung shut, a babble of voices broke out, all of them discussing him. Kendrake, yes. The new lord of the manor. Old George's nephew.

"Ivory!" Rob said sharply, making her nerves jump as she looked round at him. She had forgotten he was there. "Is that Matthew Kendrake? I've not seen him clearly before." He looked worried. "That's the man you're going to work for?"

Ivory tossed her head. "It is. So what?"

"So I don't think it's a very good idea, that's what!" Rob replied. "He's a widower, isn't he? You're going to be all alone with him at the Hall."

"Hardly alone. There'll be Janey, and Mrs. Barnes and her husband."

"The Barneses have a separate flat at the back," he said.

"And just what are you implying?" Ivory asked coldly. "That he'll only have to beckon and I'll jump into bed with him?"

Even in the dim lighting Rob's flush was evident as he avoided her eyes. "No, of course not. But I don't think your grandmother would have been happy about it—especially if she could have seen the way you were looking at him."

"Really?" Her tone had iced over. "And how exactly was I looking at him?"

"As if you fancied him."

A snort of laughter escaped her. "Oh, rubbish, Rob! I don't even like the man. From what I've seen of him, I shall be only too pleased if he spends most of his time away on business. Janey's my concern, and only Janey."

"Then why were you watching him that way? And why did you try to hide?"

"I was just assessing the enemy," Ivory said grimly.

"Enemy?"

"Yes." Regretting the annoyance that had made her indiscreet, she smoothed her hair back. "I have a feeling I'm going to find myself at odds with him over Janey. She's insecure and he's much too harsh with her. And I hid because . . . Well, because I don't want him to know what close ties I have with the village. You saw the way everyone reacted. People obviously dislike him as much as they disliked his uncle. I don't want him to think I'm part of that, or it might set us off on the wrong foot. You might ask your mother not to discuss my past with Mrs. Barnes, if she sees her."

"Well, I'm sorry. I was just anxious because you're a girl on her own now. You've got no family to stand up for you. I suppose I feel a bit responsible."

"Then don't," she said. "I'm old enough to take care of myself."

"Yes, but if it hadn't been for me, you'd never have heard that he needed a teacher for his daughter. I hope I shan't regret repeating that bit of gossip."

Ivory laughed softly, laying a hand on his arm. "If I hate it, I can always give in my notice."

Rob would never know, but she was grateful to him for passing on that particular piece of gossip. Without it, she might never have had the chance to come back to Hedley Magna. But Rob must not suspect her real motives.

Looking at his friendly, open face, she regretted having to lie to him. But if she told him the truth, he might ruin her plans. Certainly he would not approve.

She realized that he was smiling at her, his hazel eyes soft with affection. Her hand still lay on his arm, and his large paw came warmly to cover it. Flushing, Ivory pulled away. She did not want him to think she was encouraging him toward anything more than friendship.

"Will you have another drink?" he asked.

"Oh, no, I don't think so, Rob. Do you mind if we go back? I'm really tired, and there's another long drive to make tomorrow. I ought to have an early night."

"Okay, just as you like."

Outside a breeze stirred softly in the trees and dark clouds drifted across the still pale sky. Rob drove straight back to the farm. Ivory waited until he had parked his car.

"Cold?" he inquired as a shiver ran through her.

"A bit. The wind's cool."

"We'll have rain before morning," he said sagely.

Looking at him in the vague gray light, Ivory laughed. "You sound exactly like my grandfather."

"But I don't feel like your grandfather," he said, and

grasped her arm, swinging her in close to him, his lips landing awkwardly on hers for a brief moment.

Swaying off balance, Ivory stared at him in surprise. "Rob!"

"Well, what do you expect?" he said with a sheepish grin. "You come here looking like an angel when all I'm used to is grotty old cows—the four-legged variety, I mean. I'm human, Ivory. You must know how I feel about you. How I've always felt."

"We've—" She licked her dry lips, swallowing thickly to clear the sudden croak from her throat. "We've always been friends, Rob."

"Up to now. Boy-and-girl innocence. Only we're not children anymore. I thought I'd better stake my claim before Matthew Kendrake gets a chance to turn your head."

"I don't think you need worry about that," Ivory said steadily. "But . . . Listen, Rob. I like you a lot. I'm very fond of you, in fact. But I've never thought of you as—"

"I know." He thrust his hands into his pockets, watching the ground as he rocked on his heels. "But for me there's more to it. I'd just like you to start thinking of me as—well, as a man. Let's take it from there."

Ivory bit her lip, wanting to smile at his blunt, awkward way of expressing himself. "Oh, Rob," she said softly, and reached up to brush her lips against his cheek. "You're the nicest man I know."

But when she was in bed, warm and comfortable on a feather mattress beneath a sloping ceiling, with full-blown roses splashing the wallpaper and rain beginning to patter on the window, it was not Rob's image that swam through her drowsy mind. It was that of a rangy man with a lean, dark face kept very still, and with danger lurking behind bright forget-me-not eyes.

Chapter Three

When she arrived at Hedley Magna on Saturday morning, it was a relief to find that neither Matthew Kendrake nor his daughter was at the Hall.

"He's taken Janey to the seaside for the day," Mrs. Barnes explained as she conducted Ivory up the stairs. "Janey wanted to go. She's hardly been outside these grounds since they came here last March. Mr. Kendrake's very careful of her. Oh, this door leads to the master suite. Along here is Janey's room, and this is yours, next to it."

Two trips up and down the stairs accomplished the task of transferring all Ivory's possessions from her car to her room. Wearily, she sank down on the bed, pushing the damp, pale-gold hair from her eyes.

"You do look hot," Mrs. Barnes said with sympathy. "Quite a heat wave we're having. Jim—my husband— is already worrying about the garden drying out. He does the gardening, you know, and any heavy jobs. I'm sure I couldn't cope on my own. But now you're here it will be a help. Young Janey's a dear, but it's been a trial keeping an eye on her as well as doing my job."

"You needn't worry about her any longer," Ivory said.

"If I were you, I'd have a rest," the housekeeper suggested. "I'll bring you a drink and then . . . Why don't you have a dip in the pool, to cool you down?"

The thought of that shimmering blue water was too great a temptation to resist. "What a marvelous idea! Except—what time are you expecting Mr. Kendrake back? I'd hate him to come home and find me making free with his swimming pool the instant I arrive."

"Oh, I don't suppose he'd mind," the housekeeper said. "But he won't be back for a while yet. About six, he told me. He wanted to give you a chance to get settled in peacefully."

Ivory unpacked hastily, telling herself she would put her things away more tidily later, and found a yellow bikini she had never worn. It was a bit daring for her taste, fastened with thin yellow strings, and when she had it on she looked at her reflection and mused that her grandmother certainly wouldn't have approved. Still, her figure was good, and anyway, no one was going to see her.

Throwing on a terrycloth robc and a pair of flat sandals, she ventured down the back stairs to the kitchen. Mrs. Barnes was nowhere in sight, but a delicious aroma wafted from the oven. Through a half-open door Ivory glimpsed a utility room with gleaming white appliances. She walked across the tiled floor to where a glass lobby connected the main house with the back wing, which contained the flat where the Barneses lived. An outer door opened onto the lawn below the terrace.

At the far end of the pool, a white table and chairs stood beneath a big scarlet umbrella. The whole area was screened by shrubs and trees. Somewhere a tractor droned, reminding Ivory of Rob Garth. She wondered what he would say if he could see her as she slipped off the robe and plunged into the sparkling water.

She came up gasping from the cool shock of the water on her skin and struck out for the opposite side of the pool. Turning her face to the sun, she let herself float and closed her eyes against the brightness, thinking how delicious the water felt after hours spent in the heat of her car.

A shadow falling across her face made her open her eyes. She was near the side of the pool, and against the bright haze of the sunlight, a tall figure loomed darkly. He moved so that his shadow covered her eyes again, and she saw that it was Matthew Kendrake. He stood with a thumb hooked into the belt of his slacks and one eyebrow lifted into a quizzical hook.

"Oh!" Ivory gasped, letting her feet touch the bottom of the pool. She stayed close to the side, hiding her lightly clad body from his sight.

"Oh, indeed," he said lazily. "For a moment I thought you'd drowned yourself."

Ivory crouched in the pool, furiously aware of the indignity of the situation in which she found herself. "You weren't expected yet. Mrs. Barnes said—"

"I come and go as I please in my own house," he interrupted. He strolled languidly to one of the white chairs not far away, and seated himself casually. "As a matter of fact, Miss Andersen, we found the coast overcrowded. Janey was hot and I was irritable, so we came home. But don't let me disturb you." He leaned back in his chair. "I'll just sit here and enjoy the view."

Knowing full well which view he meant, Ivory flushed and wondered how she could extricate herself. Her robe lay on the chair next to her employer, her sandals beneath it. There was nothing for it but to behave as though she were used to being seen half-naked.

Ignoring his sardonic gaze, she stood up and climbed from the pool, pausing to shake back her wet hair. A trickle of water down her back made a shiver run through her, bringing her out in goose pimples, and she was suddenly aware of how closely the bikini stuck to her skin, concealing very little. Gritting her teeth, she forced herself to walk slowly to where her robe lay, keeping as far as was possible from the man whose interested gaze covered every inch of her. She threw the robe on and knotted the belt tightly, making him squint up at her face.

"You're not shy, are you?" he asked with amusement. "You shouldn't be."

Ivory turned away. "Thank you," she said stiffly.

"Oh, don't go! I've asked Mrs. Barnes to make a jug of something cool and bring it out to me after she's seen to Janey. Won't you join me? You might dry more easily if you took that robe off again. There's nothing to fear from me. I've seen women in far less than a bikini."

"I'm sure you have, Mr. Kendrake," Ivory murmured, not looking at him. "But I burn easily. I've had enough sun for one day. If you'll excuse me, I'll go to my room."

"As you please," he replied indifferently.

Ivory escaped, via the kitchen and the back stairs, where she encountered Mrs. Barnes, who told her Janey was having a rest.

"Poor lamb, she's tired out. But I've washed her face and hands to cool her. Will you keep an eye on her now?"

"That's what I'm here for," Ivory replied.

In a room whose curtains were drawn against the light, Janey lay flat on her back on the bed, dressed only in a pair of panties. Her face was flushed from the heat and she looked exhausted, making Ivory wonder what had possessed Matthew Kendrake to drag his daughter to the coast on such a day. To her dismay, Janey greeted her with an outthrust underlip and a frown.

"Had too much excitement, have you?" Ivory asked, crossing the soft carpet to the bed.

"I was all right until Daddy started shouting at me," Janey said. "It wasn't my fault I spilled orange all down my dress."

"Oh, dear." Ivory sat down on the bed, stroking the child's sweat-damp curls. "Is that what happened?"

"He said I was a clumsy brat. Only he was angry before that, too. He didn't have to go on the round-about with me. I'm big enough to ride by myself. But he said it made him feel dizzy, and he got mad at me."

How like the man! Ivory thought. "Never mind, love. I expect he was hot, too. You have a rest while I take a shower and get dressed."

"All right. Ivory, will you take me to the seaside one day? It would be better if you were there."

"We'll find lots of places to go," Ivory promised.

Standing under the cool shower, she scrubbed herself hard, as if to remove the feel of Matthew Kendrake's glance. She wasn't a prude, but he had made her feel naked. It was just further proof that he was no gentle-man.

Janey slept for an hour, then Mrs. Barnes called her for tea. Ivory supervised the child in washing and dressing, then accompanied her down to the kitchen, where the table was laid for three and Mr. Barnes sat waiting. He acknowledged Ivory's presence with a nod.

Ivory looked in puzzlement at the table. "Aren't you joining us, Mrs. Barnes?"

"Pardon?" the housekeeper said in surprise. "Oh, yes, I shall eat now. That's the usual arrangement. Janey goes to bed at seven and Mr. Kendrake dines at eight. You'll be eating with him, of course."

"With him?" Ivory repeated with a sinking feeling.

"That's what he said. But you can have a snack now, if you like."

"Oh, no. No, thank you. I'm not really hungry." She had only snatched a hurried lunch at a service station, but the thought of food was suddenly nauseating. So she had to dine with the master, did she? What devil had put that idea into his head?

"You might as well leave Janey with us for now," Mrs. Barnes said. "She's used to having her tea with us, aren't you, love? I'll send her up at seven and you can see her to bed while I get on with the dinner. Will that be all right?"

"Yes, fine," Ivory said, and returned to her room.

To be thrown into Matthew's company was not what she had expected or wanted. She had hoped to find out what she needed to know by searching through old documents and asking questions around the village, without her employer being aware of what she was doing. She had already decided there was no hurry about pursuing her quest: first she wanted to get to know Janey, but in the end she was determined to face Matthew Kendrake with the truth about his uncle's chicanery.

However, if first she had to spend her evenings alone with him, that would complicate everything. She was already aware that he found her attractive, and if she was honest she had to admit that something about his lean, muscular frame and enigmatic blue eyes made her pulse quicken in a disturbing way.

When Janey appeared, Ivory gave her a bath and put her to bed, asking if she would like to hear a story.

"No, thank you," Janey said politely. "Mrs. Barnes usually tells Daddy when I'm in bed, then he comes to say good night. We'd better do it, or he'll only get mad again."

"Then I'll fetch him at once."

She found him in the blue and gold sitting room, hidden behind a newspaper. When he heard the door open, he glanced over the top of the paper, then set it aside.

"Janey's waiting for you to say good night," Ivory told him. "I gather that's the usual routine."

He got to his feet, stretching his tall frame as if his muscles ached before tucking his shirt more firmly into his belt. "Has Mrs. Barnes told you that you'll be dining with me in the evenings?"

"Yes, she has, but—" Seeing his eyes narrow, she lifted her chin and went on firmly. "I didn't expect to be treated as a guest. I'm an employee. I'd be happy to eat with Janey in the kitchen."

"I dare say you would," he replied. "But I choose to have you dine with me. Not as a guest, Miss Andersen, but as an adult member of my household. If there's one thing I hate, it's eating alone. So you'll do me that small courtesy. Besides, since you're going to be spending your days with Janey, I dare say you'll be glad of some proper conversation."

Ivory drew a long breath and let it out slowly. "Yes, Mr. Kendrake. Do we, er, dress for dinner?"

"I certainly don't *un*dress, as a rule," he replied drily. "But there's no need to go to extremes, unless we have guests."

"I see. Thank you. Then I'll do as I am?"

"I'm afraid not. I'd prefer you to put on a skirt. I don't like women in trousers."

Ivory's eyes sparked but she bit back the retort that sprang to her lips and said, again politely, "Yes, Mr. Kendrake."

"Right." He strode toward her. "If you continue to fall in with my wishes, we shall get along famously, Miss Andersen. Now I'll go and see my daughter."

Seething, Ivory watched as he crossed the hall and climbed the stairs two at a time, his long legs carrying him with no apparent effort. He was nothing less than a dictator! she thought hotly. Imagine having the nerve to tell her what to wear!

However, since she had still to establish herself at the Hall, she decided to obey him, at least for the time being. Returning to her room, she sought out a dress that had not become too creased in the packing and found one in a light silky material in pale green. She put it on, seeing with chagrin that the neckline was rather too low for her liking, especially for dinner with Matthew Kendrake. But since her other skirts and dresses looked bedraggled from being crammed into suitcases, the pale green would have to do.

At precisely a quarter to eight a gong sounded in the hall below. Ivory went down, to find Matthew Kendrake, dressed in a gray linen suit and open-necked shirt, standing in the doorway of a room she had yet to see.

"In here," he instructed, taking a long, slow look at her from veiled eyes.

They moved into a dining room, furnished with quiet good taste, silver candelabra reflected in the surface of a table that looked as though it could seat ten in comfort. Matthew sat at the head with Ivory on his right, where a place had been laid for her, and he made conversation in an impersonal vein. They ate cold consommé, followed by roast lamb with mint jelly, and vegetables cooked to perfection. There was wine, too, which Matthew poured into crystal glasses.

Ivory sipped the wine and found it delicious. "This is very good. What is it?"

"Nothing very elaborate. A German hock I found in the cellar. My uncle kept a fine collection of wines to please his guests, but then he was a connoisseur—something I don't pretend to be."

"Your uncle?" Ivory said quietly, twirling the sparkling glass between her fingers.

"He owned this estate before me. Since he never married and therefore had no children, I was his sole heir. The last male Kendrake, that's me."

From the corner of her eye, Ivory could see his lean brown hand lying on the shining table, set off by a white shirt cuff. Across the back of it a jagged scar showed white. The last male Kendrake, he had said. And she was the last Meldrum. Between them there were old accounts to be settled.

She looked up, and saw his eyes shadowed by a somber light. "Where did you come from?" she heard herself ask, and was astonished: she hadn't intended to say any such thing.

"Here and there," was his reply. "I was born in England. But if you mean where do I call home, I'm not sure. Here, perhaps. For the moment, anyway."

Then he might be persuaded to sell the Hall, she thought. Of course, since his wife had died only six months before, he must have given up his home to come to Hedley Magna.

"You've spent some time abroad?" she asked, her curiosity aroused despite herself.

"Yes. Australia, in case you're wondering. I've developed a bit of an outback twang, haven't I? I'm a partner in a sheep station there. But I have other business interests, some of them inherited from my uncle. I don't grow roots easily." His hand flexed on the table as if he were disturbed by the personal questions. "And you, Miss Andersen? Where were you born?"

She experienced a wave of relief at the way he had phrased it, saving her from having to lie about her connection with Hedley Magna. She let her gray eyes meet his serenely. "In Kenya, actually. My father had a cattle ranch. But after my parents died I came back to England to live with my grandparents. They're gone now, too. So I suppose that leaves me without any real roots, either."

He lifted his glass, blue eyes mocking her above the rim. "Kindred spirits, Miss Andersen?"

"I wouldn't say that," Ivory said hastily. "You're obviously used to living well. My background is more humble."

"That," he replied, "is not an adjective I would have applied to you, Miss—or may I call you Ivory? Janey tells me that's your name. It's charming. Unusual. How did you come by it?"

"I've been told that my father named me. He was probably influenced by the ivory poachers he sometimes had to deal with. Apparently when I was born he said my hair was the color of old ivory, so . . ." She gave a little embarrassed laugh and shrugged.

"Your skin, too," Matthew said in an undertone, his glance caressing the smooth line of her throat and the soft curve of flesh exposed by the neckline of her dress. "Like ivory. Only softer, I imagine."

She threw up a hand to fiddle with the slim silver chain round her neck, but Mrs. Barnes' entrance to clear the plates and serve dessert saved her from having to reply. She was furious with herself for allowing the conversation to become so personal. She had started out with the intention of asking him about his uncle, but that scar on his hand had turned her thoughts to Matthew himself, for some unfathomable reason.

Chapter Four

The following afternoon, Ivory and Janey sat in the shade of the lime tree reading an adventure story. Janey read slowly, stumbling over the harder words and becoming more and more frustrated until she threw the book down and leapt to her feet.

"I don't want to read it! Anyway, it's Sunday. Nobody has school on Sunday. You can't make me—" She stopped short, suddenly dropping to the ground with her eyes on the house.

Glancing round, Ivory saw three people coming onto the terrace: Matthew, a redheaded girl wearing a brief wraparound dress, and behind them a young man whose likeness to the girl marked them as brother and sister, though his hair was darker.

"Oh, hell!" Janey muttered, shocking Ivory. "It's Carla."

"You mustn't use such language," Ivory gasped. "Where on earth did you learn that?"

Janey merely stared at her with mute defiance.

Sighing, Ivory saw that Matthew had not headed for

the poolside as she had thought but was bringing the
visitors toward the lime tree. She scrambled to her feet,
brushing at the seat of her jeans, and Janey dodged
away to run behind the one-story wing where the
Barneses had their private accommodation.

"I see my daughter's being her usual sociable self,"
Matthew said with a wry smile and a disapproving
glance at her jeans. "Miss Andersen, I'd like you to
meet Carla Forsythe and her brother Corin. Our neighbors, in a manner of speaking."

Wondering why the name Forsythe rang a distant bell
in her mind, Ivory shook hands. The redheaded Carla
gave her a withering look from green eyes, but her
brother smiled warmly, holding Ivory's hand longer
than was necessary.

"Good grief, Matthew," he said. "Nannies didn't
look like this in my day. Miss Andersen, I'm delighted
to meet you. When may I enroll in classes?"

"Don't be ridiculous, Corin!" Carla snapped. "I
thought we were here for a swim. Matthew, darling, do
change your mind and have a dip. Don't be an old
bear."

She drew Matthew away, and Ivory watched them
go. They made an attractive couple, Carla clinging
tightly to the tall man's arm, her bright hair almost
brushing his shoulder.

"I only wish we had a pool at the Manor," Corin
said, and shrugged. "Ah, well. See you later, Miss
Andersen."

As he strolled off toward the pool, Ivory saw his
sister throw off her wrap dress to reveal her golden
body clad in the tiniest triangles of white material. The
costume made Ivory's bikini seem like a coverall, and
she was sure that Carla's swimsuit would be transparent
when wet. Unwilling to be a spectator to what was

obviously a brazen invitation scene, Ivory went in search of Janey, feeling irritable.

The little girl stood on the front drive, viciously digging a deep rut in the gravel with the scuffed toe of her shoe. The fact that the gravel was showering over the red sports car that stood on the drive appeared coincidental, but Ivory knew it was not.

"Janey, stop that at once! You'll scratch the car. And you're ruining the drive when Mr. Barnes spent all morning raking it."

Janey stopped her antics, but threw back her head and scowled. "I don't care. I hate her!"

"Janey." Ivory crouched down beside the child, an arm about the thin waist. "It's no good saying you hate people. If she's your Daddy's friend—"

"She's after him," Janey declared. "Everywhere we go, she turns up. She even came out to Australia once."

"Friends do visit each other," Ivory said, but she wondered exactly what Janey meant and where she had heard expressions like "after him" spoken in such meaningful adult tones.

"I saw him kissing her!" Janey said. "On the verandah, at Wallaroola station. I was supposed to be asleep, but I saw them. And she lives near here. That's why Daddy came, so he could be near Carla."

Ivory stood up, a frown creasing her brow. Surely Matthew had not been having a relationship with Carla before his wife died. But why not—he was a Kendrake, wasn't he? The Kendrakes cared for nothing and no one. Bitter thoughts filled her mind . . . on account of Janey, and of Matthew's dead wife, who had been betrayed.

To calm Janey down, she took her for a walk in the woods that cloaked the edges of the grounds. She pointed out the different flowers and trees, using the

walk as a subtle lesson, and she thought Janey had
forgotten her temper until they returned to the house,
when the child refused to go anywhere near the back
lawns. Instead she dragged Ivory into the kitchen,
where Mrs. Barnes was busy washing vegetables.

"I made some fresh lemonade this morning," the
housekeeper said. "It's in the fridge. Help yourselves.
And, Miss Andersen, would you mind putting some in
that big glass jug, with some ice, and taking it out to the
visitors, please? They'll be glad of a cold drink, I
expect."

Ivory prepared the jug, added tinkling ice and put it
on a tray with three tall glasses. "Coming, Janey?"

The child shook her head, so Ivory went alone to the
poolside where Corin sat beneath the sunshade wearing
a pair of blue trunks. He was a little overweight, and
his skin glowed pink in patches. On the edge of the pool
his sister sat dabbling her feet in the water and watching
as Matthew swam with effortless power, drops of water
sparkling from his brown arms. So he had let himself be
persuaded, Ivory thought darkly.

"Miss Andersen, you're a mind reader," Corin said
with a grin as she set the tray on the white table. "How
did you know I was dying of thirst?"

"I'll have one, too!" Carla called peremptorily.
"Only put some vodka in mine."

"Her majesty commands," Corin said drily. "Any-
one would think she was already mistress here."

The jug seemed to slip in Ivory's hand, slopping
lemonade onto the tray. "Mistress? How do you
mean?"

"Lady of the manor. That's what she'll be when she
marries Matthew."

"I'll get the vodka," Ivory said, and hurried away.
Matthew couldn't marry that girl! she told herself

furiously, startled by the stab of jealousy that ran through her. Jealousy? Ridiculous! It was Janey she was concerned for. Didn't Matthew know what marriage to Carla might do to his daughter?

When she returned with the bottle of vodka, it was obvious that some altercation had taken place. Carla sat slumped opposite her brother with a childish scowl, and Matthew looked like a storm cloud. He stood by the table wearing a pair of brief white shorts that made his tan look even darker, his well-muscled body still glistening wet and his hair plastered round a grim, set face.

"Thank you, Ivory," he said quietly, taking the bottle from her. His fingers brushed hers, sending a jolt-like an electric shock up her arm. With one twist of his wrist he undid the cap and poured nearly a quarter of the contents into a glass, adding a dash of lemonade. "Is that about the right strength?"

"Darling," Carla purred. "You're being beastly. How was I to know your new little nanny was too precious to walk to the house and back? A servant is a servant, as far as I'm concerned."

"But do you have to drink alcohol at this hour?" Matthew returned tightly.

Ivory smiled bitterly to herself. For one mad moment she had thought he was angry on her account, but actually he was annoyed by Carla's drinking habits. It wouldn't do to have the lady of the manor addicted to alcohol.

The redhead pouted seductively. "Sorry, darling. But it's not really early. It's almost five o'clock. Share some with me, yes?" She poured half the contents of her glass into Matthew's and leaned sinuously across to add some to Corin's drink, managing to display an alarming amount of cleavage. "Let's all have some.

Does nanny want to join us? Oh, dear, we're short of a glass. Or will you take it straight from the bottle, Miss Andersen?"

"I wouldn't dream of robbing you of any," Ivory said sweetly, and turned on her heel to walk unhurriedly away. She heard Corin chuckle behind her.

That evening, when the gong sounded at seven forty-five, Ivory did not go down at once but waited until eight o'clock. Then she made her way to the dining room dressed in a simple skirt and blouse. Matthew was waiting by the door. His blue eyes narrowed as he watched her approach. Though he was fully dressed, she could not help remembering the darkly tanned skin stretched smoothly over taut muscles. Her fingers itched to know what his skin would feel like, but she curled them into her palms, shaking the thought away.

"Didn't you fancy an aperitif?" he demanded.

"I'm really not much of a drinker, Mr. Kendrake," she replied levelly. "I prefer to be in control of myself."

"So I've noticed," he said. "You kept beautifully cool this afternoon. But I can't help wondering if you ever go completely out of control."

"I seldom do," Ivory said.

"Indeed? I might take that as a challenge. But let's eat. I'm starving."

He said no more about the incident of that afternoon. He was polite, impersonal, even amusing at times, but Ivory kept herself aloof, remembering her purpose there. Becoming involved with Matthew Kendrake was not part of her plan, even though he showed all the signs of wishing to make her another conquest on an undoubtedly long list.

During the following days, Ivory's life assumed a pattern that soon became routine. She had breakfast in the kitchen with Janey and the Barneses; Matthew apparently ate a frugal breakfast in the master suite after his morning workout. Mornings were for Janey's lessons, sometimes in the playroom and sometimes in the garden, depending on the weather. They both joined Matthew for lunch, unless he had a snack at his desk in the study, where he spent most of his time. And in the afternoons Ivory played with Janey, winning her confidence and working on her education in ways the child did not realize were "school." On warm afternoons, when she was sure her employer was out— either gone riding or up to the Home Farm to see the estate manager—she and Janey splashed in the pool. Ivory hoped that learning to swim would help Janey's return to full strength.

The evenings were the most difficult. She was obliged to have dinner alone with Matthew. At those times she was most aware of the tension building under his surface politeness, and occasionally she glimpsed the dangerous man behind the bland mask when his glance flickered over her. It was like waiting for a storm to break.

One Saturday in June, a few days of cool, rainy weather gave way to blue skies and breezy sunlight. Having been housebound during the wet spell, Ivory decided to take Janey up to Top Farm to meet Rebecca. Janey appeared to be coming out of her shell, and Ivory thought it high time she made a friend near her own age. She intended to ask Matthew's permission over lunch.

But Matthew did not appear for lunch. Mrs. Barnes said he was, "Up to his eyes getting ready for a board meeting next week. He said he wasn't to be disturbed for anything, short of the house burning down. Anyway, dear, he won't mind Janey going out as long as you're with her. He just doesn't like her straying out of the grounds on her own. He's afraid she might get hurt again."

"Again?" Ivory queried, glancing toward the corner where Janey was feeding her goldfish.

"Yes. She was in an accident. Didn't you know?"

"I understood she'd been ill," Ivory said. "You mean those scars on her leg . . . I haven't liked to inquire too deeply. Mr. Kendrake doesn't take kindly to personal questions."

"I know, dear. He keeps himself to himself, doesn't he, poor man? But that's what I was told: Janey was hurt in a motor accident. Actually . . ." She lowered her voice and leaned closer to confide. "If you ask me, that was when her mother was killed, in that same accident. I've got reason to suspect that because of something I heard Miss Forsythe say. You'll have noticed that Janey never mentions her mother."

"Yes, I have."

"Well, that's why, dear. Too painful. You never know what a thing like that does to a child's mind, do you? Best not to stir things up."

Ivory looked thoughtfully at the curly-headed child who was watching her goldfish swim round his bowl. If what Mrs. Barnes said was true, it might explain a great deal about Janey.

After lunch, she and Janey set out to walk up the hill to Top Farm, using the side gate that lay opposite the old Meldrum cottage. Bright new pantiles graced the roof, and inside, plasterers and joiners were at work. Without its thatch, the cottage looked so different that Ivory could hardly believe it had once been her home.

Beneath the chestnut trees they encountered Rebecca, coming home from a ride. She slid from the pony's saddle and greeted Janey in a friendly way. As Ivory introduced the two, Janey's huge brown eyes stared wonderingly at the older girl.

"Does Janey ride?" Rebecca asked.

"Ask her," Ivory suggested.

Janey said that she did know how, but she didn't ride very well, and Rebecca generously offered the use of her pony. "Just down to the farm. And I'll have to lead him."

Janey's face was a picture of delight as Ivory helped her into the saddle, then walked alongside to make sure her young charge was secure. When they reached the farm, Rebecca offered to let Janey help her rub the pony down. "And then we can go to my room and I'll show you my toys, if you like."

Janey went off with her new friend, both of them leading the pony.

"Is that your new student?" Rob inquired, emerging from the house.

"Yes, it is," Ivory said. "I thought I'd bring her along to meet Becky."

"It's been a long time," he said, mildly reproving. "You've been here three weeks already. Haven't you had any days off?"

"No, not really. My free time comes in brief snatches. It's not like an office job."

"It sounds a bit like farming," Rob said with a grimace. "I don't get proper days off either. I've got to fetch the cows in for milking now. Are you in a hurry, or can you wait until I've finished?"

"We don't have to be back until six," Ivory replied.

Pleasure lit his freckled face. "Great! Then after milking we could go for a ride. Tansy and Pepper could do with some exercise. I suppose you do remember how to ride? Mum will look after Janey for an hour. What do you say?"

Ivory hesitated, but she had been constantly responsible for Janey for three weeks without a break, and now that she was away from the Hall—away from

Matthew Kendrake—the pressure seemed less intense. "I'd love to, Rob," she said eventually.

Once up on Tansy's back, Ivory discovered that her brain had not forgotten the techniques of riding, though her muscles were out of practice. She rode with Rob to the woods behind Hedley Hall, where the horses trod carefully along a well-marked bridleway. Sunlight dappled down through swaying leaves and birds flitted among the branches. Somewhere not far off, a cuckoo called.

"So how are you enjoying the new job?" Rob asked.

"I'm beginning to make progress," Ivory said slowly. "Janey's mixed up, but there are signs that I'm getting through to her."

"And her father?"

Surprised, Ivory looked across and found him frowning at her, speckled sunlight playing across his tousled hair. "What about him?"

"Do you see much of him?"

"No, not really. He closets himself in the study when he's not out somewhere. We meet at lunch and dinner, but then we usually talk about Janey's progress. Why?"

"Just wondering," Rob said, a stubborn look on his face.

Ivory knew very well what he was wondering, and she resented it. It was none of his business what went on between her and Matthew Kendrake—not that anything was going on that she could put a name to. But even if they had been embarked on a wild affair, Rob had no right to make any comment or disapprove, as he clearly did.

She watched the damp earth of the bridleway where marks of other hooves were imprinted after the rain, then suddenly drew Tansy to a halt. "I think we'd better go back, Rob."

"Why?" he demanded. "We've hardly been out twenty minutes."

"I know, but I don't want Janey to get overexcited. She's my responsibility. Besides, my legs are starting to ache. I'd forgotten how hard riding is on the thigh muscles."

Rob sighed and said grudgingly, "Oh, all right. But you'll come out again, won't you? You've a right to some free time, time to see your friends."

"I'll see what I can arrange," she said.

They turned back along the woodland path and were almost in sight of the road when Ivory saw, with a pang of dismay, the rangy figure of Matthew Kendrake strolling towards them. At the same moment he recognized her and his brows came down in the now-familiar frown.

"Where's Janey?" he demanded, striding to stand at Ivory's stirrup with one hand on the reins, his dark head flung back as he frowned up at her.

"She's perfectly safe," Ivory assured him, disturbed by the anger glowing in bright blue eyes. "I've left her with Mrs. Garth at Top Farm."

"And who the hell is Mrs. Garth to have charge of my daughter? What do you think I'm paying you good money for? Go back and fetch her at once."

Rob nudged Pepper forward, saying, "It's all right, Mr. Kendrake. My mother will—"

"You stay out of this!" Matthew snapped. "Did you hear me, Ivory? I want Janey back at the Hall within half an hour. If any harm's come to her—"

"Would I have left her if I'd thought she would come to harm?" Ivory flared, furious with herself for her physical awareness of him, the hand near hers on the rein and the brown column of his throat disappearing into an open-necked shirt. "What do you take me for?

Very well, I'll go and bring her straight home. I just thought it might do her good to be let off the leash for a while. And me, too!"

Stabbing her heels into the horse's flanks, she set it to a gallop that made Matthew step back as she rode headlong for the road, pausing only long enough to make sure the way was clear before making for the farm track. Behind her, Rob rode to catch up. But he failed to reach her until she was sliding from the saddle in the farmyard.

"I'll have to leave you to rub her down, I'm afraid," she said, brusque with anger.

"But . . . You're not going to let him get away with that, are you? You've got a right to some free time."

"So you keep saying!" she cried. "Oh, don't talk to me, Rob. I'm ready for a fight, and if I stay here I'll fight with you."

She rushed into the farmhouse and found Janey peacefully tucking into homemade bread and jam with Rebecca. Apologizing to Mrs. Garth, Ivory explained that they had to leave. Janey didn't want to go, which meant more argument, and by the time Ivory managed to get the child outside they were both ill-tempered. But Rob was waiting with his car to drive them back to the Hall.

Taking a deep breath, Ivory forced herself to calm down as the car bumped up the track. "Thanks, Rob. I'm very grateful."

"That's what friends are for," he said, giving her a sidelong look. "But I'm none too happy about this whole thing. He may be paying your wages, but that doesn't mean he owns you. Since when has he been calling you by your first name?"

"Since I gave him permission to!" Ivory exclaimed. It wasn't exactly the truth but she was too furious to care.

"I see," Rob said flatly. "I see."

"You don't see at all," she retorted. "You never did see further than the end of your nose, Rob Garth."

He was silent, concentrating on his driving until he pulled up by the Hall gateway. "This do you?"

"Yes. Thank you," Ivory said stiffly, helping Janey out.

As Rob drove away, she thought bitterly that this was another point to score against Matthew Kendrake. Now he had made her quarrel with Rob.

The argument in the car had stilled Janey's tantrums. She looked up at Ivory with worried brown eyes. "What's the matter, Ivory? Did I do something wrong?"

"You?" She bent swiftly to hug the child. "Oh, Janey, love, no, it wasn't your fault. I shouldn't have taken you out without asking your Daddy first. But you've had a good time, haven't you? Do you like Becky?"

Janey nodded. "Will Daddy let me go to play with her again?"

"Yes, I expect so. But next time we must ask him."

Holding Janey's hand, she walked up the curving drive. Her steps slowed as she saw her employer waiting on the porch. On either side of him the clematis was in full bloom, drifts of pale pink and rich purple against the golden stonework. She quickened her pace and marched on toward him, pretending to be unaware of the demon she saw leaping behind his eyes.

Before either of them could speak, Janey burst out nervously, "We had a wonderful time at the farm! There's a girl called Becky. She let me ride her pony, and we saw the cows being milked and then I had some bread and jam."

The stern lines of his face softened a little as he bent to ruffle his daughter's curls. "You're hot, Janey. Go and wash your face."

Janey rushed away, apparently relieved to be away from him.

In silence, Matthew stepped aside so that Ivory might enter the house. She would have gone after Janey, but he stopped her. "You should have told me about these 'friends' of yours. Perhaps I'm being over-protective, but you don't know what . . ."

Very slowly, Ivory swung round to look at him, tensed against the quickened thud of her pulse. "I'm only sorry you think so little of my judgment, Mr. Kendrake. I was responsible for Janey, and in my estimation she was entirely safe with Mrs. Garth and Becky. But of course if you don't trust me, then in future I shall make sure I have your permission before I treat her to anything outside her usual routine."

One dark eyebrow lifted derisively in a way Ivory found quite maddening. "Before you let her off the leash, in fact. Isn't that the way you put it?"

"The best way to help her get back to normal is to allow her a normal life!" she replied. "She needs friends of her own age. Making her feel like a prisoner is no way to restore her confidence."

His glance traveled over her with an arrogant intimacy that made her flush. "And you feel that I'm keeping you a prisoner, too?"

"Yes, I do, if you want the truth!" she cried, alarmed by the effect that the look in his eyes was having on her nerves.

"A prisoner? Locked up? Totally in my power?"

"That's the way it feels!"

She started to move away, but his hand on her arm prevented her, making her freeze. It was the first time he had touched her. Even through the sleeve of her shirt the feel of his fingers made her flesh burn, sending out sparks that invaded her whole body. His cool blue gaze swept slowly across her face, noting every detail of the snapping gray eyes and the full lips, now set with stubbornness.

"My prisoner?" he murmured. "No, not yet, Ivory. But don't tempt me."

She tried to jerk free, but his fingers only tightened on her arm, making her heart thud erratically against her ribs. Inwardly quaking, she managed to say scornfully, "Is that what you learned in Australia? I've heard they like their women subservient out there. But here in England—You wouldn't dare!"

Before she could move he had locked one arm about her waist, holding her in close to him as the other hand cupped her chin. The devil gleamed at her from his blue eyes as he bent very slowly and touched his lips to hers with sensual intent.

The shock of that first contact made Ivory's stomach turn over. Her brain began to spin. She felt herself wilt, her resistance melting as he kissed her softly, his lips moving on hers until they parted of their own volition under the unbearable sweetness of his assault. As she relaxed against him, his hand caught in her hair, stroking it and at the same time holding her captive.

Something inside her protested. But her body refused to answer the call to resist, and her blood seemed to flow like warm honey as her arms slid round him.

Abruptly, he lifted his head to stare down at her with glazed blue eyes, breathing unevenly. He said in a charged undertone, "Wouldn't I dare, though, Ivory? Just try me!"

"And what would your precious Carla say to that?" Ivory spat, determined not to let him see how deeply he had affected her.

"Carla?" His voice was dangerously soft, his gaze fixed on her tender mouth.

"Yes, Carla! Your future wife!"

Glinting blue eyes snapped back at her with sudden menace. "Who told you that?"

"Corin did."

"I see. And do you really think it's any of your business?" His hands pressed her even closer to his body. There was no mistaking the fact that he, too, had been roused to fever pitch. She had never experienced such feelings before. They frightened her, partly because of the anger she now read in his eyes. Frantically she sought for some way to bring him out of this lustful mood.

"It's my business when it concerns Janey!" she flung at him, and was relieved when the steel muscles in his arms relaxed a little. "Do you know that Janey hates Carla?"

All at once the threatening glower left his face. His eyes turned glacial and he released her, stepping away. "Yes, I'm aware of that. But I'm afraid that, if and when I decide to marry again, I shan't consult my daughter first."

She was left staring at the study door, which quivered from the furious slam he had given it. She was appalled that he could discount Janey's feelings so callously— and even more appalled when she remembered how she had melted against him, her senses scrambled by his physical proximity. Her mind detested him, but her body had responded with disgusting alacrity.

To a man like that! To a Kendrake!

Chapter Five

In the morning, Ivory sent Janey out to play in the grounds, then found herself wandering nervously about the house expecting at any moment to encounter Matthew. But there was no sign of him.

"Oh, didn't he tell you?" Mrs. Barnes said in surprise when she brought coffee out to the terrace where Ivory sat in the shade. "He's gone to London for this board meeting. Be away for some time, so he said. That's why he was so busy yesterday, trying to get the estate business straight. Mr. Firth's a good manager, but Mr. Kendrake likes to know exactly what's going on."

That was probably why Matthew had been in the woods yesterday, Ivory thought. He'd been coming back from a visit to Angus Firth, the estate manager, who kept his office at the Home Farm. Pure bad luck had caused all that trouble. She recalled how it had ended, with herself locked in Matthew's arms, and a flush heated her entire body—with shame, she knew. How he could have gone off to London without a word to her or Janey would have been a mystery, if she hadn't known that that was the kind of man he was. Having virtually told her that she must not take Janey anywhere without his permission, he had put himself out of reach. Did he really expect her to stay at the Hall patiently awaiting his return? Despite his threats, she was not his prisoner, nor was Janey.

That Friday evening, Ivory received a phone call—from Rob Garth.

"I'd have come to see you," he said, "only I didn't want you to get into trouble again because of me. Is there any chance you might get away tomorrow? There's a local gymkhana and fête. Becky's taking part, on Cherry. I wondered if you'd like to come."

"We'd love to, Rob," Ivory said, pleased. "I'm sure Janey would enjoy it."

"Oh; Janey," he said, then sighed. "Can't you get away on your own?"

"Not at the moment. Mr. Kendrake's away on business. Besides, Janey would love to see Becky riding in a gymkhana."

"Well, all right," Rob said dubiously. "I'll pick you both up about two o'clock. Okay?"

"I look forward to it," Ivory said. "Do I gather I'm forgiven? I didn't expect you to speak to me again after—"

"Oh, I've forgotten all about that. It wasn't your fault, it was that, that *boss* of yours. I'm glad he's gone away. See you tomorrow, then."

The prospect of seeing a gymkhana excited Janey. All morning she asked questions and was impatient for Rob to arrive. Ivory had dressed both Janey and herself casually in denims and T-shirts, with sweaters in case the weather grew cool. For herself she had added sunglasses and a broad-brimmed straw hat to protect her face from the sun.

Rebecca and her pony were already installed in the competitors' area of the big field where horse-boxes stood in rows and children in jodhpurs and protective hard hats fussed over their ponies. Lines of flags fluttered in the breeze and around the jumping ring, which was marked off by ropes. All manner of tents and stalls had sprouted beneath the oaks and elms.

They watched Rebecca win her class and proudly claim her cup. Then the girls wanted to try all the games: throwing bean bags, smashing plates and bowling. Laughing, Ivory and Rob watched their antics. She was delighted to see how well Janey and Rebecca got on together. Janey seemed so different from the sullen, difficult child she had first encountered.

Rob must have been thinking the same thing. "She's not such a bad little kid, is she?" he said as they found a relatively quiet corner of the field and sat down, the girls giggling over ice creams and rolling in the long grass. "I don't know why her father doesn't send her to school. That's what she needs, from the looks of her: a normal life."

"But if he sent her to school," Ivory said, "I should be out of a job again."

"I know." He turned his head to look at her, the wind ruffling his fair hair. "That's what I was thinking. Ivory, why don't you marry me? I know we could be happy. It's what I've wanted for ages. And Mum's all for it."

Feeling trapped, Ivory swallowed the lump in her throat and was thankful that her sunglasses disguised her expression. "You've discussed it with your mother?"

"Yes, of course I have. She knows how I feel about you. She said I was to stop messing about and do something positive for a change. I know you're not madly in love with me, but that kind of thing doesn't last. I'd settle for affection, for the time being. I'd take good care of you, Ivory, you know that."

"But, Rob," she managed, and was interrupted by a voice from somewhere above her head, a deep male voice saying satirically, "What a delightful rural scene!"

"Daddy!" Janey exclaimed, leaping to her feet. "Oh, Daddy, this is Becky Garth. She's my best friend."

Janey's intervention gave Ivory time to stand up and compose herself, though she felt shaken by the rush of joy that had filled her at the sound of his voice. Fiddling with the sleeves of the sweater she had tied round her waist, she drank in the sight of him. He wore casual slacks and a shirt with the sleeves rolled up and the buttons undone, but he looked tired, with fresh lines drawn on his face and a weary shadow clouding his eyes even as he spoke pleasantly to the children. She had a crazy impulse to throw her arms about him and kiss away those lines of weariness.

Janey was demanding hot dogs and Matthew gave her some money, saying, "Just don't make yourselves sick," as the two girls darted away. Then he slowly turned his head to look at Ivory. "Mrs. Barnes told me where to find you."

"We, we weren't expecting you home yet," Ivory faltered, pushing the sunglasses farther up her nose.

"I'm aware of that," he said evenly, his glance flicking over her, lingering momentarily on the outline of her breasts beneath the T-shirt. "You're getting sunburned. Put your sweater on."

Ivory glanced down at her arms, seeing that he was right; her skin was reddening even though she had kept to the shade as much as was possible. Untying her sweater, she slipped it on. But as she shook out her hair, she caught Rob's eye and saw his moody, suspicious look.

"I do burn easily," she said defensively.

"I know that," Rob muttered. "I've known you for most of your life. Remember?"

Ivory stared at him, belatedly recalling that he had just proposed to her. And she hadn't given him an answer.

"Aren't you going to introduce me to your, er, friend?" Matthew said quietly.

"Yes, of course. Mr. Kendrake, this is Rob Garth. He lives at Top Farm. He's Becky's brother."

Matthew held out a hand. His narrowed eyes perused Rob, who hesitated for a moment before sticking out his own hand.

"Now that I'm here," Matthew said smoothly, "I can relieve you of the trouble of taking Ivory and Janey home. I'm grateful to you for looking after them for me, Mr. Garth, but I'm sure you have other things to do."

His gaze locked with Rob's. The young farmer stood with clenched hands and set jaw, but eventually backed off from a confrontation. "Yes, I've got to get the horse-box back to the farm. I'll . . . see you soon, Ivory."

As he strode away, Ivory watched him unhappily, wondering why she had let Matthew walk in and take charge so easily. There ought to have been something she could say, some protest that would have put him in his place as her employer, not her keeper. But in fact, she had not been anxious to prolong her meeting with Rob. Matthew had rescued her from what might have proved to be an awkward situation—though he needn't have done it so high-handedly.

"I had no idea he was a friend of such long standing," Matthew said, tilting a quizzical eyebrow. "Did he say he'd known you most of your life?"

"Yes, we—" She hesitated, glad of the sunglasses

that hid her confusion. She could hardly say she had lived in Hedley Magna since she was four years old, or he might guess the rest. "His family were friends of my grandparents. Rob and I have . . . kept in touch."

"How nice for you," Matthew said mockingly. "I hope I didn't interrupt anything just now."

Her nerves all stood to attention. The need to practice deception irritated her. "Only my day off," she said shortly.

"You've been able to try your wings for a whole week now," he replied, one corner of his mouth lifting wryly. "I understand you've been making the most of my absence by taking Janey out for trips. Along with your old friend Rob Garth?"

"He's much too busy with his farm," Ivory retorted. "Anyway, those outings were educational."

"Naturally, you being so conscientious in your work. There's no need to go on the defensive, Ivory. I have no objections to your taking Janey out. Last time I was angry only because you left her with strangers."

She opened her mouth to say that the Garths were not strangers to her, but the memory of how that day had ended made the words die in her throat. And something about the way Matthew was looking at her told her that he, too, was recalling their last encounter.

"I'd better go and find Janey," she said hurriedly.

"Yes, do that. Bring her to the car. It's quite near the gate."

There was no escape from having dinner with him that night. As she came down the stairs, he stood in the dining room doorway lazily surveying her loose summer dress.

"That's better. Why do you spend your days in those hideous jeans? They're so unfeminine."

"They're comfortable," Ivory said. "And they're practical. I'm a teacher, not a decoration." She paused in front of him, waiting for him to move aside. But instead he leaned casually against the doorjamb.

"You could be both, if you tried," he said in a low voice. "In fact, you accomplish the miracle without trying. You're—" The phone rang sharply in the hall and he broke off, swearing under his breath. "I'll get that. Tell Mrs. Barnes to start serving."

Wondering exactly what he had been about to say, Ivory sat at the table as Mrs. Barnes ladled out soup. She could hear Matthew's voice, though his words were not clear, and she awaited his return nervously, fearing the trend of that broken conversation. In a flattering mood, he could be formidable. She had not forgotten how easily he had made her respond to his kisses. Every time she was near him she felt tense and prayed that he would not touch her. If he did, her bones might turn to jelly again.

But when he came back, he had apparently forgotten what he had been saying earlier. He took his place at the head of the table with a curious glint in his eye.

"We've been invited to a party."

"We?" Ivory said in disbelief.

"You and I. That is, Carla is inviting me and Corin is inviting you. A Midsummer's Eve dinner party, at Meddlingham Manor. I said we would go."

Her eyes widened as she remembered why the name Forsythe had seemed familiar. Meddlingham Manor was the home—the stately Elizabethan home—of Lord and Lady Forsythe. Carla and Corin must be their offspring.

Midsummer's Eve arrived. Bathed, perfumed and groomed, Ivory stood in front of her long mirror and wondered if she had gone a fraction too far. The dress was a clinging white sheath with a bow-tied halter neck, the skirt split up the side to well above the knee. Over it went a voluminous cloak of silky diaphanous material that shimmered with gold and bronze lights. Her grandmother would not have approved.

On the other hand, Ivory mused, turning this way and that as she lifted her arms to watch the effect, it was very subtle. With her hair caught up in a silver-gold coronet and her makeup echoing the colors of the shimmer, she looked as though she belonged at Hedley Hall—the last of the proud line of Meldrums. Her ancestors would have visited Meddlingham Manor without a second thought, and now so could she. She felt that they would be proud of her.

In delicate gold sandals, she left her room and went down the stairs. Matthew stood in the hall, lean and elegant in evening dress, his thick hair still unruly despite the attentions of a comb, and his skin very dark against a brilliant white shirt. Ivory moved slowly, aware that he missed nothing of the sight she made. She saw his blue eyes flare as he drew a sharp breath, then his expression was veiled again, as was hers. She daren't risk him knowing that she longed to be clasped against that white shirt, to let her fingers tousle his hair even more.

"A pity," he said with a slight shake of his head. "A long dress. It's a shame to hide your legs."

"Is that why you object to trousers?" she asked boldly.

"On you, yes."

Exhilarated by the effect she was having on him, Ivory lifted her arms and slowly spun round, allowing him to see one slender leg beneath the split dress. Matthew's face was expressionless when she faced him again, but she was aware of the tension beneath that carefully arranged blankness. For once she did not fear the hidden desire in him but welcomed it as the beginning of her triumph. She could use it for her own ends.

She smiled shyly at him, her gray eyes sparkling behind long, dark lashes. Tonight she was a Meldrum. Let all Kendrakes beware.

"You're ready for our little charade, are you?" he said abruptly, turning to open the front door. "Let's go."

As they approached the door to Meddlingham Manor it opened to reveal a uniformed butler, who bowed and announced their names to the gathering in the vast hall. Around the stairs and in the adjoining rooms, beneath vast pictures in gilded frames, people laughed and chatted over drinks, the men all in evening dress, the women wearing bright colors and glittering with jewels. Matthew's hand beneath Ivory's elbow guided her into one of the rooms where antique furniture and cases of china were set off by long velvet drapes. More people stood or sat, glamorous and wealthy, making Ivory feel out of place.

"Matthew, darling!" Carla in a swirl of shocking pink with a large expanse of tanned midriff showing, her red hair decked with pink flowers, rushed over to them. She ought to have looked horrible, Ivory thought, but to her chagrin, the effect was stunning.

Beside the vividly dressed girl, Corin beamed at Ivory with boyish delight.

"I see you've brought nanny," Carla said with a laugh, though her green eyes darted hatred at Ivory. "We'll let Corin look after her. Come over here, darling. I want you to meet some people."

And she dragged Matthew away. Corin claimed Ivory's arm.

"I'm so glad you could come," he said, drawing her toward an alcove where drinks were being served. "I've been frightfully busy or I'd have been over to the Hall to see you before now. It's too bad of Matthew to keep you all to himself."

"He doesn't," Ivory said. She glanced behind her, but Matthew and Carla had disappeared into the throng. "I'm just his employee."

"Not tonight you're not," Corin said stoutly. "You're my guest. And you look simply marvelous. What would you like to drink?"

For a few minutes Ivory let a strange misery have its way with her. But then Corin's flattering attentions restored her spirits. Matthew, after all, was a grown man and should be able to cope with Carla. What did he expect Ivory to do? She could hardly separate him from the redhead without appearing to be jealous, and that she certainly was not. The very thought was ludicrous. She didn't want Matthew Kendrake. Let him fight his own battles.

She smiled at Corin and allowed herself to enjoy his open admiration. But every now and then she sought out Matthew's dark head, visible wherever he happened to be in the room since he was one of the tallest men present. He appeared to be thoroughly enjoying himself. And so would she.

Dinner was served in a vast dining room still boasting its original Elizabethan paneling, ornately carved and darkened by time. Three sets of French windows had been left open to the sunset, a warm breeze drifting in to flutter the candle flames as the guests sat down at two long tables. Ivory found herself beside Corin, unable to see Matthew. Occasionally she heard Carla's high-pitched laughter above the murmur of conversation.

A different wine was served with each course, and soon Ivory found herself flirting with Corin, her inhibitions vanishing on a cloud of euphoria.

Afterward, she could never quite remember how she came to be in that dark arbor. Most people drifted into the gardens after the meal, to smoke cigars or simply enjoy the scent of moonlit flowers during a stroll around the twining walks and stepped pathways. Music floated from the house. Somehow Ivory found herself in the shelter of a summerhouse, where Corin had his arms round her and was kissing her enthusiastically. She seemed to remember clinging to him with a kind of desperation, as if willing him to take away the memory of Matthew Kendrake's warm lips and hard arms.

Then someone else appeared out of the shadows, someone who forcefully separated her from Corin and laid an iron hand around her wrist to drag her, stumbling, to a car. Blinking hard in a vain attempt to clear her head, she watched the trees rush past with the moon sailing behind them as the car drove swiftly along country lanes.

She sat up and put a hand to her head, which seemed about to fall off her shoulders. "Nobody asked you to rescue me."

"You weren't sober enough to ask." Matthew seemed about to explode with anger. "Good grief, in another few minutes he might have—"

"He wouldn't! I'd have stopped him."

"How? By passing out? You were incapable of stopping a child on a tricycle."

Sighing, Ivory let her head roll onto the rest above her seat. "Don't go on at me, Matthew. I'm tired."

"You're drunk as an owl!"

She squinted up at him in the drifts of silver light. "Do owls get drunk?" She imagined a family of owls hiccupping and cross-eyed; bubbles of laughter rose up and shook through her. It seemed the funniest thing ever.

She was still laughing helplessly when the car stopped. Her door opened and Matthew pulled her out, none too gently.

"For heaven's sake!" he said tightly. "What's so funny?"

"You are!" Ivory spluttered, trying to move away. But the ground wouldn't stay still and she stumbled against him, feeling the world spin as he held her close, steadying her.

"Ivory!" he muttered in a voice that shook. His lips sought hers feverishly and he nibbled a burning trail across her cheek to her earlobe and the soft area beneath it. "Ivory!"

Her body began to respond to him and she clung to him tightly, borne away on the magical tide. All thoughts of repulsing him vanished; her fingers buried themselves in his thick wavy hair and smoothed his strong shoulders.

His firm mouth possessed hers again, her lips parting on a sigh of delight. He folded his arms round her and kissed her deeply and she pressed closer to his warmth, her fingers caressing his ear and cheek. She was lost in the sensual power of his hands and mouth and the hard warm body so close to her own she could feel his desire for her matching her own needs.

She moaned as his hand found her breast, her senses all alive to him. The Meldrums could go hang. She wanted Matthew Kendrake to make love to her.

Suddenly he lifted his head, his eyes blazing down into hers as he held her arched against him like a pliant willow and she stared back at him with helpless pleading, her pupils dilated, her mouth swollen and soft with desire.

"Thanks for the invitation," he said gruffly, "but make it again when you're sober."

Feeling sick with shame, she turned and ran for the

house, tears stinging her eyes as she wondered what on earth had possessed her to lead him on that way.

She took a shower as hot as she could stand, hoping to rid herself of the wanton female who had led her astray. Far from revenging herself on him, she had let Matthew work his devilish spell on her senses. She hated him. Hated him! So why—oh, why?—was he the only man who could make her bones melt and her blood run like hot wine? It didn't happen with Rob; it hadn't happened with Corin. Only Matthew Kendrake could make her feel totally alive.

Chapter Six

She kept to her room the following day, telling Mrs. Barnes and Janey that she felt unwell. It was true enough; her head felt like concrete and her stomach was in revolt. Her appearance was convincing, too: a face paler than usual, with dark shadows under haunted gray eyes that stared at her from the mirror, asking questions that were impossible to answer.

Matthew sent Mrs. Barnes up with some vile concoction in a tumbler, and a message that it would do her good.

"Overdid it last night, did you?" the housekeeper said with a laugh. "Well, we're all entitled to kick over the traces once in a while. You'll be all right. Just take it easy today."

Ivory drank the brew, which didn't taste as bad as it looked. She thought bleakly that if it had been poison she wouldn't have cared. Thank heaven Mrs. Barnes didn't know how very much she had "overdone" everything last night. She rested all day and didn't get up until Janey was in bed.

Downstairs in the sitting room she found Matthew

brooding over a glass of scotch and scribbling something on a pad. He glanced up in surprise, laid the pad aside and got to his feet, frowning.

"You look like a ghost. I didn't expect you down. Will you have a drink?"

"I think I've signed the pledge," Ivory said with a tight, humorless smile. "I don't want anything to drink, or any dinner. But I've got to talk to you."

"Of course. Come and sit down."

"I'd rather stand, if you don't mind. Mr. Kendrake, I want to give you my notice."

"Oh, yes?" he said calmly, that maddening eyebrow quirking. "Why?"

"You know why! After last night—"

He dismissed last night with a negligent wave of the hand. "That was an aberration. You were drunk and I . . . I wasn't too sober myself. Let's forget it."

Ivory did not believe her ears. Forget it? Pretend that nothing had happened, when she was shamed to her soul?

"You can't possibly leave us," he said reasonably. "What about Janey? She's just beginning to find her feet. She needs you. Do you seriously intend to desert her?"

"She—she can go to school, proper school, after the summer holidays. She'll soon catch up."

"She's not ready for that yet."

Clenching her hands, Ivory said desperately, "We did agree to a three-month trial. Obviously it isn't going to work. Besides, I—I'm going to get married."

He seemed to wince, and momentarily a frown creased his brow. Or did she imagine it? Quite casually, he said, "Yes, I think you should."

"Then you agree?" she said breathlessly, wondering if she had understood him. "But you said—"

"I said you couldn't leave us. And you can't. I won't

allow it. But when you're my wife you won't want to leave, will you? There'll be no reason for it."

Blood rushed to Ivory's head and drained away, leaving her swaying. Marry him? Marry Matthew Kendrake? No, never! To be his wife . . . But she couldn't. She wouldn't! And yet . . .

"Your wife?" she managed. "*Your* wife?"

He reached to set his drink on a table and came slowly toward her, taking her cold hands in his warm ones, so that her mind became even less coherent.

"After last night, you can't tell me you wouldn't like that, Ivory," he said quietly. "You must be aware that I find you extremely attractive, too. Consider: you'd be mistress of Hedley Hall, wife to a wealthy man, mother to a little girl who loves and needs you."

"And what about Carla?" she asked hoarsely.

"Carla is a little too mercenary and demanding for my taste. You're more careful. I like a thrifty woman, though I'd make sure you had everything you could possibly need in the way of clothes and jewelry to suit your position."

It sounded like heaven, she thought dazedly—not the clothes and jewelry, but to be Matthew's wife. But the dregs of her common sense made her say, "You can't be serious. Marriages aren't made like that."

"I assure you a lot of them are, though usually the real reasons are covered up under a lot of nonsense about love." He released her hands and stepped away, returning to the table to sip from the glass of scotch. Then he said in a hard-edged voice, "I suppose you would have been happier if I had said I love you, but whatever else I may be I'm not a liar. I'm incapable of feeling love. You may as well know that."

He sounded as though he meant it. His voice and the cold expression on his face made him seem like a man of granite, impervious to softer feelings. But of course,

Ivory thought, it was barely seven months since he had lost his first wife. He was still grieving, that was all. And perhaps he meant that no one would ever replace Janey's mother in his heart.

"On the other hand," he added, "I'm a normal man with normal desires. I happen to feel that a clear understanding is preferable to a lot of romantic non-sense, an understanding entered into while both parties are in full command of their mental faculties, not floundering in pink clouds of emotion. Or would you have me believe you're desperately in love with your worthy farmer?"

"Rob's a good man!" Ivory said, bridling in defense of her old friend. "He's kind, and honest—"

"And industrious, reliable, and dull," he finished for her. "The sort of man you could twist round your little finger. Is that really what you want?"

"He loves me!"

His lips twisted cynically. "That word again. How original! And you? Do you love him? No, don't bother to answer that. I know the answer. You gave it to me last night. You would never have thrown yourself at me if you had felt any deep devotion for your estimable Rob Garth."

She felt her face flame. Did he have to keep reminding her about that? "I wasn't myself."

"Well, that's a euphemism I could argue with. A nice way of saying you were plain old-fashioned sozzled. If you weren't yourself, Ivory, then who were you? Drink loosens the inhibitions; it doesn't alter the basic person-ality. You were just begging me to take you, and if you'd been sober I'd have been happy to oblige. Which is how I know we'd be better off married to each other. Why don't you go to bed and think about it? I'll have Mrs. Barnes bring up a tray. You look as though you need an early night."

Late into the night Ivory lay awake turning over the proposal in her mind. She couldn't do it, she told herself. It was impossible.

But she couldn't marry Rob, either. She was too fond of him to accept everything he offered without being able to give something in return. Matthew—damn him!—had been right: she couldn't live with a man as compliant as Rob.

Nor could she simply leave Hedley Magna and abandon Janey, who had learned to trust her. To Janey she had become one of the few stable things in a bewildering world.

Tossing restlessly in the darkness, she thought about Matthew, that complex, dangerous man whose mere glance could make her feel vibrantly alive. Of course he wanted her, physically. She had known that for a long time. But he couldn't be as cold and hard as he pretended. No human being could, not even a Kendrake. She recalled the underlying bitterness she sensed in him at times, and it puzzled her. He was an enigma, a dark, brooding mystery with a devil behind forget-me-not eyes, but he could make her ache inside.

A phrase he had used kept repeating insidiously in her mind: "mistress of Hedley Hall." How ironic it would be if she, a Meldrum, were to return to her ancestral home as the wife of a Kendrake. It would be a victory of sorts, a reclamation of Meldrum rights. But somehow her quest had lost its urgency, and she doubted that she could submit to marriage simply in the cause of justice.

Eventually, as dawn grayed the sky, she fell into a deep, exhausted sleep. But later she was dragged out of troubled dreams as a small body flung itself onto her bed and thin arms fastened round her neck.

"Oh, Ivory! Ivory, wake up! Isn't it wonderful!"

"Janey!" Blinking away layers of sleep, Ivory untangled the arms that threatened to strangle her and sat up, staring at the child. "What time is it?"

"Late. I had my breakfast ages ago. Mrs. Barnes told me to stay away, but I just had to see you." Brown eyes danced with joy as she bounced on the bed. "I'm so happy. Are you?"

"About what?"

"That you're going to be my stepmother!" Janey cried, flinging herself into Ivory's arms. "Daddy told me. It's super news, isn't it?"

Stunned, Ivory held the child close to her, pleased that Janey couldn't see her face. Matthew had told his daughter? Without waiting for an answer?

"I'm going to tell Mrs. Barnes," Janey said, leaping from the bed. "And then I'm going to find Mr. Barnes and tell him. Can I be a bridesmaid and have a pink dress? I've always wanted to be a bridesmaid in a pink dress." She skipped out of the room, humming to herself.

Ivory hastily took a shower, threw on a shirt and jeans and went in search of Matthew. He was in the blue and gold sitting room, occupied again in scribbling on a pad. How he could sit there calmly making notes at a time like this was beyond her. She slammed the door, making him look up.

"You're wearing those damn jeans again," he said with a sigh.

"I shall wear what I please!" Ivory stormed. "Why did you tell Janey we were going to be married? She's over the moon! It's nothing short of emotional blackmail."

"I thought you might need a push in the right direction," he said, laying the pad face down on the coffee table.

"So you did tell her on purpose? Oh, you—you're impossible! I suppose you've forgotten telling me that if you planned to marry again you wouldn't consult Janey first?"

He eased himself out of the chair. Even that simple movement reminded her of the lithe muscles hidden beneath skin that felt like warm silk. "I didn't consult her first," he pointed out. "I consulted her second, after you."

"Now you're splitting hairs! What are you going to tell her if I turn you down?"

"Nothing, because it won't happen," he said with the utmost confidence.

"What makes you so sure of that?"

"I've seen you with Janey. You care about her. So you won't destroy her dreams. Are we going to continue this shouting match, or shall we discuss it like civilized adults?"

It was really too funny for words, Ivory thought angrily. He had completely turned the tables. *He* was blackmailing *her* into something which she had half planned to do anyway. Since he was so cold-blooded about it, it made her decision easier.

"Let's be civilized by all means," she said flatly. "Let's discuss this 'clear understanding,' as you call it. Understand that if I marry you, it will be for Janey's sake. I'll be her stepmother, and mistress of this house, and if you wish I'll keep Carla Forsythe at bay. But that's all, Matthew. A marriage of convenience. A wife in name only. Is that clear enough?"

As he strolled toward her she stiffened, her chin high and her hands clenched so he couldn't see that she was trembling. She felt impaled by his blue gaze, mesmerized by the wicked demon that lurked there taunting her. And all the time some treacherous part of her was straining to be close to him, preventing her from running away.

His hands lifted to cup her face as if it were a fragile

flower. He bent to kiss her softly, expertly, gauging the exact pressure needed to draw a response from depths over which she had no control. A trembling started deep inside her; she heard herself sigh; her hands stole up the front of his shirt. His arms came round her, arching her in against him while his fingers ran lightly up her spine, making her moan and shiver.

Then he lifted his head and looked at her with a mocking smile. "Your famous cool keeps slipping, Ivory. We'll see how long you can stand being 'in name only.'"

She wriggled to be free, but he only pressed closer. Seeing that he was enjoying the movement of her body against his she became still, glaring up at him, though her own body was reacting violently. "I can stand it longer than you can!" she hissed at him.

Laughing sardonically, Matthew released her. "We'll see about that. Go and ask Mrs. Barnes to make coffee, will you?"

"Go yourself!" she cried, furious that he could affect her so deeply, so easily, and seem untouched himself.

"Oh, very well," he agreed pleasantly. "Any little courtesy that will please my fiancée."

As the door closed behind him, Ivory shook her fist impotently, breathing names she had not learned from her grandmother. He was a devil, a monster . . . a Kendrake!

And he had given the last of the Meldrums a chance for sweet revenge. She would deny him his physical satisfaction. It was really that simple. Except that she wasn't at all sure she could do it to him—or to herself.

She was obliged to act a part most of the time. Janey talked of weddings and asked questions about the service and what would happen afterwards, and Mrs. Barnes, though surprised, seemed equally pleased.

"I've always thought he needed another wife," she told Ivory. "He's not the sort of man to be alone too much. He needs a woman's tenderness."

Ivory wondered how the housekeeper could have reached such an inaccurate conclusion. Matthew needed nothing from a woman except the use of her body. He had made that clear when he talked about the "nonsense" of love.

Something that troubled her a lot was the thought of Rob's reaction to the news of her forthcoming marriage. She could not imagine how she would ever explain it to him. Whatever she said, Rob was going to be hurt. Although she owed it to him to tell him the news herself, she hesitated. She was afraid that he might see through her excuses and perhaps try to talk her out of such madness.

One evening at dinner, she was dumbfounded when Matthew set a velvet ring box on the table beside her, opening it to show her the beautiful square-cut emerald. The sight of the ring made a nervous pulse throb in Ivory's throat.

"What's it supposed to be?" she asked flippantly. "A mark of ownership?"

"It's usual for a man to buy his future wife an engagement ring. I promised not to keep you short of anything. I'm a wealthy man. But you know that."

Meeting his eyes, she said steadily, "Do you think I'm a fortune hunter?"

"I wouldn't be surprised," he replied. "You knew all about me before you ever came for that interview. Your friends at Top Farm had told you—via Mrs. Barnes, of course. Not that I'm complaining. I admire a girl who can use her initiative."

"I'm flattered. But if you think I came here with ideas about cajoling you to the altar, you couldn't be more wrong," she said, her gray eyes steady on his.

Matthew's smile didn't reach his eyes. "I think I believe you. But you still used your initiative to get yourself a job. I was deeply impressed."

"You liked the look of my legs," she said ironically.

"Yes, I did. And the rest of you isn't half bad, either. I've always liked beautiful women. And beautiful paintings, and fine wines."

"You have a collection of all three, no doubt," she suggested. "Paintings on your walls, wine in your cellars, and women—where do you keep them? Hidden discreetly in love-nests?"

The blue demon smiled enigmatically. "If you expect me to incriminate myself, I must disappoint you. How many men have *you* left in the lurch, apart from young Garth?"

"Hundreds. But . . ." She hesitated, discarding her flippancy. "Rob's the only one who matters. He deserves an explanation. I shall have to go and see him."

"No need," he said with a wave of his brown hand. "I've already done that. I called at the farm a couple of days ago."

"And told him what?" Ivory demanded.

"The truth: that you and I are going to be married quietly at the beginning of next month. I've invited him and his family to the reception. I thought you'd like to have some friends present."

Astounded by his nerve, she struggled for words. "And what did he say?"

"He said he hoped we'd be very happy. He told me to be good to you. Then we shook hands. It was all very civilized, very stiff-upper-lip. He even introduced me to his mother. I've asked her if she'd mind looking after Janey while we're away on honeymoon. That will give the Barneses a break, too."

"You had the cheek—" she choked. "Your arrogance defies description, Matthew. You had no right to go there on your own. They're my friends. You might have let me tell them in my own way."

"What, tell them you're marrying me because of Janey? I couldn't allow that." His fingers clamped over her left wrist possessively. "Besides, I won't have you going to visit old boyfriends. You're mine now, like it or not."

She stared into blue eyes that were intense and fathomless, almost hypnotizing her, and for the first time she admitted to herself that she feared him. For Janey's sake she had to go through with this marriage, and for old wrongs that could only be avenged when a Meldrum came back to Hedley Hall. But she was afraid of the man who was going to be her husband. He had threatened to make her his prisoner and now he had accomplished his purpose. He desired her body without caring for the damage he might do to the person inside it.

On the evening before the wedding, she had to endure a dinner party with the Drummonds. Harry Drummond was a close business colleague of Matthew's, and he had brought his wife with him to attend the wedding. Ivory received their good wishes with the peculiar kind of numbness that had been settling over her for the past few days. Harry Drummond was a solid, pleasant man, his wife Nancy pretty and smiling, but nothing of the conversation penetrated Ivory's mind. She knew she had performed her part adequately, and if she had been a little quiet, it had been put down to the natural nerves of a bride on the evening before her wedding.

Still feeling as though she were moving in a dream, Ivory ate the special breakfast Mrs. Barnes brought. On the tray there was a card in an envelope addressed in Rob's handwriting. The card had a picture of a demure bride and handsome groom amid showers of orange blossom, white doves and silver bells. The verse was trite, referring to the joys of the bridal day and the wedded bliss to follow; it made Ivory wonder what Rob would say if he knew there was no love involved in this match to which she was about to commit herself.

She faced herself in the mirror as she applied the lightest of makeup. Her skin was pale as alabaster, even her lips bloodless; her gray eyes stared back at her bleakly. She emphasized them with shadow and liner, and colored her lips a pale pink, then, as an afterthought, smudged a touch of lipstick on her cheekbones to make herself look less like a ghost.

Since it was to be a registry office wedding, with no church service, she had chosen a dress and jacket in a creamy jersey silk, with a wide-brimmed hat made of stiffened lace. The pale outfit complemented her coloring and she felt that she looked like a bride, except for the emptiness in her eyes. But she would have to summon a smile for the sake of other people, for darling Janey and dear Mrs. Barnes, and for the Drummonds.

She heard a car drive away, and a few minutes later Janey rushed in, wearing the pink dress she had dreamed about, her curls brushed and shining and her brown eyes dancing with excitement.

"Daddy and Mr. Drummond have gone," she announced. "Mrs. Drummond sent me to ask if you're ready. You do look pretty, Ivory. Are you coming? We don't want to be late."

Touched by Janey's innocent pleasure, Ivory bent and kissed her cheek. Whatever happened, she could not regret that she was making Janey's life secure. Hand in hand, they went down to the sitting room.

She accepted the glass of sherry Nancy Drummond brought her and walked to the window to look out through the break in the trees, across the rolling fields. Lifting her glass in farewell to the past, she murmured under her breath, "For Janey. And for the Meldrums!" and drank the sherry in three quick gulps.

It did help, she supposed. She felt a little lightheaded as Nancy Drummond drove along the lanes toward Grantham, the quiet market town where the ceremony was to take place, while Janey chatted merrily from the back seat. The Drummonds would act as witnesses. Ivory thought that it was probably just as well that she had no father to do the traditional thing and ask if she had any last-minute doubts.

Arriving at the registry office, they were shown into an anteroom where Harry and Matthew rose to their feet, both wearing dark suits and gray ties. But there the resemblance ended. Harry, homely faced and tending to paunch, beamed his delight. But Matthew seemed forbidding, tall, tanned, and about as relaxed as a coiled spring. His dark face showed all the warmth of a carving. In his eyes the devil was somber, watchful, making Ivory wonder how she had ever come to this moment.

But here it was.

Then it was over; the words said, the signatures written, the kiss exchanged—a cold, formal kiss. Was he as apprehensive as she was?

His lips felt like ice, chilling her.

Chapter Seven

The sleek car purred round the drive of Hedley Hall and eased to a halt. Matthew let Janey out, then walked round to open Ivory's door and offer his hand.

"Go and open the front door," he said to Janey, who rushed off to the porch. Then he bent and swept one arm behind Ivory's knees, the other beneath her shoulders, and lifted his bride into his arms. She clutched for the cartwheel hat, but it fell off and floated to the gravel. Matthew ignored it.

"There's no need—" she began, and was silenced by a look.

"Put your arms round my neck," he ordered. "I'm going to carry you over the threshold. We may as well do the thing properly."

Ivory obeyed, watching his strong profile, the straight nose and firm line of his jaw, his mouth clamped shut making hollows under his cheekbones. Her lips ached to be pressed to his throat as he carried her effortlessly across the gravel.

"I didn't know you were a romantic," she jibed.

"Yes, let's do it properly. The form without the meaning, the words without the emotions."

He stepped through the porch and into the hall, where he stopped and turned his head to look at her squarely. "And now the kiss," he said under his breath.

"Yes, master," she muttered, and leaned forward to let her mouth meet his erotically, determined to have her victory at this moment.

Matthew let her feet drop to the floor and his arms clasped round her, one hand caught in her hair to keep her imprisoned. My husband, she thought as the magic of his proximity worked its usual damnable spell, making her lean weakly against him.

He held her away from him, his eyes glinting with mockery. "Welcome home, Mrs. Kendrake."

Only then did she realize that they had an audience. The Drummonds laughed in the porch, and beyond the open door of the drawing room, where a buffet table was bright with flowers, stood the Barneses, Mrs. Garth, Rebecca, and Janey—and Rob. Coloring, Ivory looked at the man she had married, and hated him. The triumph was his, after all.

Small though it was, the reception was another ordeal for Ivory. Harry Drummond insisted on making a speech in which he made several coy references to the wedding night to come; toasts were made and clichés spoken. And all the time Ivory was bitterly aware of how uncomfortable Rob and his family felt.

"It was lovely of you to come," she said to Mrs. Garth, meaning it. "And I do hope Janey won't make too much extra work for you. I had no idea Matthew was thinking of asking you to have her while we're away or I'd have—"

"We're only too pleased," Mrs. Garth said. "Becky's looking forward to it. Janey's a little dear. You're not to worry. You go away and enjoy yourselves." But her eyes were saying "How could you do this to my son?"

At last Ivory forced herself to turn to Rob. "Thank you for the card. It was sweet of you to think of it."

"I wanted you to know there's no hard feelings," Rob said awkwardly. "We'll still be friends. If ever you need me, you know where I'll be. Thanks for inviting us, but I think we'd better be off now. I've got chores to do. We'll . . . see you around, I expect."

"Yes, of course," Ivory said, whispering so that her tears didn't sound in her voice. She was sorry to have hurt him, sorry that he and his mother seemed to feel she was now somehow out of their reach.

They left swiftly, taking Janey with them. Ivory was alone with her husband and the Drummonds. Harry and Matthew, standing by the buffet table, were talking business.

"Have some more champagne," Nancy Drummond suggested, coming to fill Ivory's glass as she stood by the front window, staring down the drive. "Those are nice people, those friends of yours. It was good of them to have Janey. Matthew'll be relieved she's in such good hands."

"Yes," was all Ivory could think of to say.

Soon, the Drummonds left. Ivory went to her room to prepare for their journey, while Jim Barnes stowed the cases into the car. Matthew had been very secretive about their honeymoon destination, telling her only that it was to be in England: "I've had enough of flying for a while. You'll need clothes suitable for the English climate and the country life." When she came back to the Hall she would no longer be sleeping in this airy room but in the master suite—in the master's bed. But he would find no joy with her, if she could help it. It would be the days that would make her life worthwhile, days spent making Janey feel secure and loved, and days when at last a Meldrum would be mistress of Hedley Hall again. Why, suddenly, did it seem such a hollow victory?

Then the door suddenly opened and Matthew walked in, carrying her cartwheel hat. Ivory gasped and began to protest at his invasion of her last few moments of privacy.

"I'm your husband now," he said laconically. "Or had you forgotten?" He held up the hat. "Do you want this?"

"No, I don't think so. Leave it."

Tossing the hat onto the bed, he came to take her by the shoulders, his fingers urgent through the soft material of her outfit. "Not having regrets, are you, Ivory? It's too late for that. You're mine, and I intend to make sure you stay mine."

"That ought to work both ways," she said dully. "Or did you think I'd turn a blind eye to your affairs?"

"Just give me ample reason and I'll be faithful," he replied, pulling her into his arms and kissing her gently.

Ivory sat beside her husband as he headed the car north up the broad sweep of the A1 highway. She glanced at his hands, tanned and capable on the wheel, wearing no ring to mark him as a married man. On her own hand the thick gold band and the emerald felt heavy, a constant reminder that she belonged to him. But there was nothing about him that said he belonged to her.

"Where did you get that scar on your hand?" she asked.

He was frowning against the brightness of the sun, but flicked a glance at her distractedly. "Scar? Oh, tangling with some barbed wire. Get the map out and navigate for me, will you? We want York for a start. We'll stop there and have a cup of tea."

Glad of something to do with her mind, Ivory consulted the maps and wondered if he had given her the job to stop her from talking. He didn't need a navigator; the road went practically all the way to York and the signs were clear enough.

From the city of York, with its ancient walls and solid cathedral, they drove through pleasant vales and villages with country mansions on their outskirts, to Pickering, the small town backed by the dark bulk of the North York Moors. They could be heading for the coast, Ivory thought, or perhaps there was some fabulous hotel hidden in the wilds, offering riding and walking facilities. The thought cheered her, for she loved the wild loneliness of the area, having spent a holiday there one summer. It would be a small compensation for the loveless marriage to which she had condemned herself.

When they stopped for a snack, Matthew studied the maps, not allowing her to see which particular place he was looking for. He stowed the maps away in the glove compartment and said he knew where he was going; she could relax and enjoy the scenery.

After a while, Matthew turned down a side road that wound tortuously into a shadowed valley with lonely farms dotting the rugged landscape and dry-stone walls draped like lacy shawls across the flanks of the hills. Then they began to climb again, along a dirt track so little used that grass grew down the center.

"Where exactly are we going?" Ivory asked. "There can't be any hotels this far in the wilds."

"Who said anything about a hotel?" Matthew replied with a cold smile. "You'll soon see."

At length, as the light faded, they came in sight of a

low stone building with a slate roof, standing alone in a
hollow sheltered by sycamores, with a stone wall
marking the edges of the property. Matthew stopped
the car outside the house and produced a set of keys
from his pocket.

"Honeymoon Cottage," he said drily. "At least,
that's what we'll call it from now on. We're going to be
entirely alone for two whole weeks. Let's take a look at
the place, shall we?"

He opened the door and flicked on a light. Ivory saw
a big kitchen with low dark beams, a scrubbed wooden
table and the usual appliances, including a big refriger-
ator freezer that, she saw when Matthew opened it, was
fully stocked.

"I've never asked you if you can cook," he said.
"Now we'll find out."

All the walls were whitewashed, with black-framed
prints hanging on them. Stairs angled up from a small
hallway, and there was a sitting room furnished in dark
oak and chintz, with a big open fireplace laid ready with
logs. It was a comfortable, friendly, welcoming place;
in different circumstances Ivory might have loved it.
Now she was filled with apprehension as her husband
led her up the stairs.

They found a bathroom, a small bedroom with a
single bed, then opened the third door and stepped into
the main bedroom. Hovering nervously in the doorway, Ivory saw a simple wooden bed covered in a
crocheted coverlet of rainbow colors, with furniture of
polished oak and bright rugs on the floor.

"Lovers' nest," Matthew said in an undertone, flicking her a wicked look. "Right, Mrs. Kendrake. I'll
bring the cases in. You make a start on supper."

Ivory found an apron in a drawer in the kitchen and
put it on over her pale dress. The cupboards contained
everything she might need, and in the deep-freeze she

discovered homemade pies and bread, carefully labeled, as well as meat and prepared vegetables.

"Who does this place belong to?" she asked as Matthew appeared with the luggage.

"To us, of course," he said with a surprised lift of eyebrows. "It was my uncle's favorite retreat."

Touched by the way he had said "us" and not "me," she said, "But who looks after it? All this food, it's been specially prepared."

"I arranged it that way. The Wheelers down at Beck Farm keep an eye on the place. Mrs. Wheeler keeps it aired and cleaned, and when somebody's due she stocks up with food and her husband gets the generator going. Who did you think did it, the little people?"

"I just wondered. What would you like to eat?"

"Something quick. I'm absolutely starving." He disappeared and she heard his footsteps on the stairs.

She chose a precooked steak pie, frozen french fries and mixed vegetables. This wasn't quite the way she had imagined this evening would be. At least she had something to do to take her mind off the coming night.

When Matthew came back, he had changed his wedding suit for navy slacks and a white sweater. He searched the pantry and emerged, smiling, with a bottle of wine. "Good old Uncle George. I knew he'd have a store somewhere."

Looking askance at the bottle, well aware of the effect its contents might have on her determination to resist him, Ivory asked, "Haven't you been here before?"

"Never had the chance," he said, clattering in a drawer in search of a corkscrew.

"But you used to visit Hedley Hall when your uncle was alive?"

"Not very often, not after I went to Australia. Why?"

"I never—" she began, and bit her lip. Matthew mustn't suspect she had lived most of her life in Hedley Magna, so how could she say she had never seen him there? She was sure to have remembered him; those lean good looks might have turned her girlish head.

Luckily he was too preoccupied to inquire into her bitten-off sentence. But Ivory had visions of him at the Hall as a guest of his uncle's. Was that where he had met Carla?

"Ah, there it is," he sighed, turning with the corkscrew in his hand. "Red wine needs to breathe before it's served, you know. If you've finished what you're doing, why don't you go and put on something more comfortable?"

"Oh yes, *sir*," Ivory said tartly, and escaped. Although the kitchen was large enough, it seemed small with Matthew in it. His head almost touched the low beams and his vibrant presence filled the whole room with electric sparks that jumped along her taut nerves.

She was horrified to discover that he had unpacked her suitcase as well as his own and distributed the clothes into drawers and wardrobe. Her dresses hung alongside his suits in a curious intimacy. And across the bed, draped invitingly, lay a nightdress and negligee that she had not seen before. Made of delicate silk and lace, it was a seductive outfit. Her pale skin would shine through the sheer weave. Was he expecting her to appear for supper in those flimsy items?

Without even touching the nightdress, Ivory hurriedly changed out of her formal wedding clothes and slipped on a pair of jeans and a loose blouse. She would have liked to delay her return to the kitchen, but a glance at her watch told her the food would soon be ready.

Matthew sat at the table, pouring wine into two

glasses. His mouth tightened when he saw her attire, but Ivory ignored him, her pulse jumping, and went to open the oven and check the pie. It was almost done; the french fries were hot.

"It won't be cordon bleu," she said over her shoulder, "but at least it's quick."

She was aware that, while she dealt with the final preparations for the meal, he was watching her. Nerves made her fumble. The pie was nearly burned when she took it from the oven. She served the food onto two plates, giving him the much larger share, and took them to the table, seating herself at the far end from him.

"Just as well we have Mrs. Barnes to cook for us at the Hall," Matthew said drily.

"You said you were in a hurry," she retorted. "If I'd had the time, I could have done something fancy. But then you didn't marry me for my culinary ability."

"No." That single word managed to convey all manner of intimate nuances, and made Ivory flush and reach for her wine glass. Over its rim she saw Matthew watching her with a baleful light in his eyes.

"I assume you put on those jeans to defy me," he said. "Didn't you like your wedding present?"

"Wedding present?" she repeated lightly, frightened of the ominous tension that suddenly lay like a blanket over the cottage. "Oh, is that what it was? Thank you. Yes, it's beautiful. But it hardly seemed suitable for the kitchen. You did say I was to wear something comfortable. I'm most comfortable in my old jeans."

His lips stretched in a slow, wolfish smile that made her aware of how totally alone they were. He looked as if he knew exactly what was in her mind but wasn't bothered: he was confident of his own ability to override her, however she might plan to stall him.

Thoughts of the coming night, alone with him in that

country bedroom, made her pick at her meal. She began to feel that if she ate another mouthful she would be sick.

"If you're not hungry," Matthew said eventually, "why don't you go to bed? You must be tired. I'll clear up in here, after I finish this wine."

The bottle was still half full. Ivory had sipped a little from her glass but wanted no more, for fear of what it might do to her. Now she feared what it might do to Matthew.

"Yes, I am tired," she said, rising from her chair, wondering what to say next. If she bade him good night he might laugh, for she would be seeing him shortly—seeing him, and having him touch her in the way he had every right to touch her now. She stood there uncertainly for a moment, her gray eyes wide with apprehension. Then she ran up the stairs to the bedroom.

She bundled the filmy silk and lace negligee into a drawer and put on one of her own cotton nightgowns, wondering if she dared bar the door. There was no lock on it, but if she set a chair under the handle it would provide a barrier. But Matthew was capable of breaking down such a barrier, and then he might take her in anger.

Eventually, she sat on the bed, unwilling to climb between the sheets. But the night air was cold, and soon made her shiver. She put out the light and lay down, huddled into a ball of misery. Perhaps if she were asleep when he came in, he might leave her alone.

Desperately, she sought sleep. But the more she tried to force herself to unconsciousness, the more wakeful she felt. Moonlight lay silver against the chintz curtains; outside, the wind breathed through the sycamores. Every little sound made her tense with panic as timbers creaked in the roof. Somewhere a sheep bleated and a night bird called, emphasizing the vast emptiness of the moors surrounding the cottage.

With no apparent transition, she found herself waking up. Moonlight had been replaced by sunlight. In disbelief she looked at the other pillow: it remained uncreased, plump and laundered to perfect whiteness. Matthew had not come to bed.

She sat up, rubbing her eyes like a child, wondering what game her husband was playing now. Why hadn't he come to bed? Had the wine put him to sleep at the kitchen table?

The cottage seemed so quiet that she leapt out of bed and threw back the curtains in alarm that Matthew might have abandoned her. But the silver gray Mercedes still stood in the yard.

When the door clicked, Ivory swung round, one hand holding tumbled hair from her face. Matthew came in, fully dressed, bringing her a cup of tea. He looked fit and full of energy, as if he had slept soundly.

While she stared at him speechlessly, he let his gaze run slowly over her with open appreciation, then lifted his eyes to her face again and said, "Are you aware that with the sun behind you that nightdress is practically transparent?"

Ivory swiftly stepped away from the window, causing Matthew to smile.

"I thought you were going to sleep all day," he added. "I've already been for a long walk. I'm going to make a start on breakfast now. What would you like?"

"I'll—" she began, and found a nervous catch in her throat. "I'll make it for you. Just let me get dressed."

"I'm quite capable of making breakfast," he replied, setting the cup down on a side table. "Are you hungry?"

"No, not really. Just some toast."

"If you're sure that's all you want. Personally, I'm ravenous. Must be this clean air. Come down when you're ready." And he left her.

Ivory stood quite still, unable to believe her senses. He had made no move to touch her. And apart from that comment about her nightdress, he had behaved as if she were a stranger. It was what she had wanted—so why did she feel so bitterly disappointed? At the sight of him, she had experienced a dreadful longing to be in his arms.

Then she recalled what he had said on the day she accepted his proposal of marriage: "We'll see how long you can stand being 'in name only.'" Now he was putting her to the test. And he was confident that he would win.

Furious, Ivory told herself that she would not give him the satisfaction of showing him how much she wished to be made his wife in every sense.

Chapter Eight

The silent battle went on. They walked together on the moor and went driving, visiting the town of Whitby with its cliffs and picturesque harbor; they took a trip on the North York Moors steam railway and generally behaved like tourists. But he never touched her, not even the lightest brush of hands. And as four days went by, the tension between them increased.

Matthew slept in the smaller bedroom. He had moved most of his clothes into there, without explanation. Neither of them had mentioned their unconsummated union.

On the fifth day of their honeymoon, Matthew left her alone in the cottage while he went down to the valley to see about hiring some horses for the following day. By mid-afternoon Ivory was unable to bear the solitude. She set out for a walk on the moor.

The wind swept the purple heights, tugging at her sweater and jeans, making her hair stream behind her in a pale gold banner. Tears stung her eyes as she thought of the nine more days she must endure of this farce. Matthew was inhuman, made of icy rock. If only he said he loved her, even if it was a lie. If only he would be warm and tender, she would give him anything.

Stumbling into a hollow, she lay down and wept bitterly, wishing she could find some way of escaping this marriage. But there was no escape, not without risking further emotional damage to little Janey.

A damp chill made her look up. She was enclosed in a bank of mist that had swept in from the coast to blanket the heights. Aching from the storm of tears, she got stiffly to her feet and stared with sore eyes at the opaque walls of fog that surrounded her, shifting and deceptive. Turning back in what she hoped was the right direction, she began to pick a way among the heather, looking for familiar landmarks. But each few square yards of the moor looked exactly like the rest. To her increasing horror, she couldn't be sure where the cottage lay.

Before long she realized that she had come the wrong way. By now she should have reached the valley. But as she stumbled on, there was nothing but hummocks and gullies covered by the purple carpet of heather and marked by odd outcrops of rock. It was bitterly cold. Moisture dampened her hair and face and began to penetrate her clothes. With rising panic, she realized she was lost.

Then she heard a voice calling her name. Matthew's voice!

"Matthew!" she got out through chattering teeth, caring about nothing but that he should come. "Matthew!"

She felt weak with relief when he appeared through the mist. His long legs rapidly closed the distance between them; his face was taut with anger—or it might have been concern.

"What did you come out in this weather for?" he demanded.

"It wasn't like this when I left the cottage," she said wearily. "I didn't realize . . ." As she took a step towards him her knees buckled and he stooped to catch her, holding her against his jacket. His brilliant blue eyes devoured the sight of her wan face as if he were a starving man and she a banquet. Then he dropped his mouth to hers and kissed her, with a desperate passion that made her senses swoop as she clung to him.

Without a word he lifted her into his arms and began to carry her back the way he had come, to where the mist thinned and drizzle seeped from the underside of the clouds. She clasped her arms round his neck, shivering, her cold lips resting on the place where a pulse beat in his throat. All she could think was that she was safe—safe because Matthew had come.

Orange flames from the log fire lit the gloom in the sitting room. He laid her on the settee and she heard him pound up the stairs. A few moments later he was back, bringing his own thick bathrobe.

"You must get out of these wet things," he said hurriedly, pulling her sweater up. She obediently lifted her arms, too cold and weary to protest, and he pulled the sweater off. He undressed her briskly, as if she were a shop-window dummy, stripping her of the jeans he so hated and then of her underwear before wrapping her in his warm robe. He brought a towel and rubbed her hair vigorously, then made her lie down on the cushions while he knelt beside her, drying his own hair. It was left in damp, spiky ends that made him look endearingly youthful.

Numbly, Ivory watched his dark face, her own face deathly pale with shadows under her gray eyes. Then Matthew's fingers stroked her cheek, feeling warm and curiously tender against her skin; his thumb brushed her lips, his gaze following the movement with aching hunger. A tremor seemed to run through him, and then he bent over her and warmed her mouth with the heat of his own. She threw her arms around his neck, burying her fingers in his damp hair, holding him as she kissed him without reserve.

Her name was an agonized whisper on his lips as he laid a hand against her throat and pushed aside the bathrobe, leaning to kiss her bare shoulder. Lightly as a butterfly his fingers moved over her, making her tremble with longing, her body beginning to cry out for him. He unerringly answered her needs, stroking her breasts until they tingled, gently opening the bathrobe, until she lay naked under his gaze, his hands and mouth working the powerful spells that she no longer wished to deny.

She moaned when he drew away and stood up. But his burning blue eyes held hers as he threw off his own clothes and returned to lie beside her, the naked length of his body warm and hard against hers as he kissed her with more urgency and she wrapped her arms about him, stroking the ridged muscles of his shoulders and back. She could feel the desire in him mounting, days of self-denial suddenly rushing them both to a peak of shared pleasure and delight. Ivory heard herself cry out. But after brief pain there was glory, and her inner volcano erupted with shattering force.

Afterwards they lay together quietly on the big settee, his head on her breast while her fingers played with strands of his thick hair and the world settled back into place. He sat up and began to pull on his clothes, while Ivory watched him, feeling very tender towards him. Strange, complex man that he was, he had been gentle with her, and for that she was grateful.

He stood up and looked down at her, his gaze

caressing every inch of her white body. But when his eyes met hers again, they were as cold as winter lakes.

"So you won," he said in an odd, hoarse voice.

"Matthew!" Drawing the bathrobe round her, Ivory sat up, a hand stretched out to him. "There wasn't any fight."

"Wasn't there? We've been engaged in war ever since we've been here, Ivory. But you've got your victory. I gave in first."

"We both gave in," she amended worriedly.

He swung round and knelt by the fire to add another log, then watched the sparks rise up the huge chimney.

"Matthew." She reached out to touch his shoulder, fresh tears stinging her sore eyes. "I love you."

"There's no need to lie," he said harshly.

"I'm not!"

Suddenly he was on his feet, towering over her with a face as grim as Nemesis, and now the demon in his eyes threw scorn at her. "I told you once before: love has nothing to do with us. Love only blinds you and makes you vulnerable. So don't kid yourself. You don't love me. You merely enjoyed my lovemaking. That's fine; that's all I ask of you. There's nothing wrong with enjoying each other physically. But for God's sake don't burden me with protestations of love. I don't want them or need them."

Ivory hugged herself, suddenly feeling like something used and tossed aside as she stared at the fire through a glaze of tears. "What did she do to you, the woman who made you feel this way?"

He made no attempt to argue with her accurate guess, but said roughly, "She made me a laughing-stock."

"And you think I'll do the same?"

"I don't intend to give you a chance. You may as well go to bed and rest. You look like a drowned rat."

Her eyes were wide with pain as she looked at him, appalled that he could say such a thing. Only a few minutes before he had gazed at her as if she were the most beautiful creature in the world, and now . . . How could he be so cruel?

"Oh, go upstairs!" he grated, turning his shoulder to her as he leaned on the mantelpiece.

Not daring to speak for fear her tears would betray her unhappiness, she hid her face from him, got up from the settee and walked to the door. But something made her pause, controlling herself with an effort as she turned to ask, "Who was she, Matthew? I think I have a right to know."

"She was the woman I was stupid enough to marry nine years ago," he replied, watching the fire.

"Janey's mother?" she breathed.

"Just so. Janey's mother." When he swung round his face was almost ugly with contempt. "And I don't intend to discuss it—not with you, not with anybody."

She held onto the door, looking like a big-eyed child lost in the roomy folds of his bathrobe, her feet bare and her hair tangled. She didn't care if he saw her tears now. "I'm sorry, Matthew."

"For God's sake!" he roared at her. "Don't give me your pity."

She fled to her bedroom and lay shuddering on her bed, tormented by memories of tenderness that had been destroyed by deliberate cruelty. She had offered him her heart and he had rejected it. It was not a thing she would offer twice.

Exhausted after sleepless nights and the morning's traumas, she fell into a troubled sleep. Hours later, she awoke with a head that felt like lead and limbs that ached. Rain still dripped down the window and the light was gray, but her watch told her it was late afternoon. Time to be thinking about making something for dinner, something special that would celebrate, if that was the word, the consummation of their marriage. Despite his harshness, she remembered the way he had made her feel earlier. When she thought of the coming night, the same fire ran through her veins. Perhaps she could make him forget his first wife.

On the table in the kitchen there was a jewelry box, and a note. She opened the box first and was thrilled by the sight of an emerald pendant that matched her engagement ring. Thinking that Matthew had repented his harshness, she snatched up the note and opened it, seeing the slashing black handwriting that typified him. It said, "Telegram from Harry Drummond. Urgent business. Will walk down to Beck Farm for a lift. Keys for the Hall are in the car, if you want to go home. Sorry. Matthew."

Ivory read it three times before the truth sank into her stunned mind. He had gone. Just like that. That casual "Sorry" was like a blow across the face. And the pendant, what was that—a bribe to keep her sweet, or a reward for services rendered? How dare he walk out and leave her?

She shut the jewelry box and tossed it into the nearest drawer, slamming the drawer so hard that it shook. She ran up to the smaller bedroom and found all his clothes gone, and his suitcase. Not a trace of him remained in the cottage. He had packed his things, and gone, without even bothering to wake her to explain.

She sank down onto the settee where only a few hours before she had been taught what physical love could be like. Physical it had been, and only that, for him—and perhaps for her, too. Perhaps he had been right when he said she had simply enjoyed his lovemaking. She couldn't believe she would be stupid enough to fall in love with a man as heartless as Matthew Kendrake.

Having endured one restless, lonely night in the cottage, she packed her belongings into the Mercedes and drove down to Beck Farm to inform the Wheelers that she was leaving. Mrs. Wheeler seemed most concerned at the abrupt ending to the honeymoon. She said that Matthew had seemed distracted the previous afternoon, but her husband had driven him to the station to catch a train for London and she hoped it wouldn't be too long before Ivory and her husband returned to the cottage.

Driving the Mercedes was easy once she accustomed herself to the controls. It had automatic gears and traveled effortlessly along country roads and highways, giving her plenty of time to muse over Kendrake callousness. For a while she had allowed her relationship with Matthew and Janey to distract her from her original intention, but now she was determined to fulfill the vow she had made to herself: not just to regain the Hall, since she was already its mistress, but to find out the truth so that she could prove to Matthew that his "good old Uncle George" had been little better than a thief.

By mid-afternoon she was driving through the gates and up through the trees toward Hedley Hall. She would be alone there, with the Barneses off on a well-earned holiday and Janey at Top Farm, but for the moment she preferred it that way. There were things she had to do.

She installed herself in the master suite, which had its own sumptuous bathroom and dressing room with fitted wardrobes and drawer units. The bedroom was spacious, decorated in autumnal shades of brown and tan with splashes of orange. This is your home, Ivory told herself. Meldrums belong here. You're mistress of Hedley Hall.

Having stopped to buy essential provisions on her journey, she soon made herself a meal and had the washing machine churning merrily in the utility room. But her mind was on the study, which remained locked as it always was unless Matthew was working in there. She had a feeling it might contain clues that would help in her search for the truth.

Presumably Mrs. Barnes had a key, since she must clean the study. But Ivory could not find the housekeeper's keys; the Barneses' flat was securely locked. Telling herself that she had every right to look through her own husband's belongings, she returned to the master suite and made a systematic search of the dressing room. Eventually she found what she was looking for: a small bunch of keys, casually tossed into a handkerchief drawer.

As she went down the stairs, she began to feel uneasy. Matthew might be angry if he knew she was using his absence to spy on him. Except that she wasn't spying on him, not exactly; it was his uncle's activities that interested her. She promised herself she would not pry into anything unless it had some connection with George Kendrake.

The study was tidy; the big desk held only a blotter, a tray for pens, and a telephone. Ivory walked round the room, breathing in the scent of wax polish and old books. One wall was filled entirely with bookshelves on which a variety of volumes rested. There was a swivel chair behind the desk, a row of filing cabinets, and near the window, a leather couch stood by a low table. Outside, the trees stirred in the evening breeze.

Looking at the bunch of keys in her hand, she tried

some of them in the lock of the filing cabinet. But access to it only showed her copy files connected with Matthew's business interests, particularly Kendrake Enterprises, of which he was chairman. The letter heading named Harry Drummond as managing director, which was interesting information but not what she was looking for.

She turned to the desk and stood for a moment frowning over the doodles on the blotter: flowers, trees, and one tiny sketch that looked like Janey. She had not suspected that her husband had a talent for art. But when she unlocked the drawers, her search proved fruitless. There was nothing that had any connection with George Kendrake.

Sighing, Ivory locked the desk. Perhaps there was no evidence left. It was, after all, forty years since her grandfather had had to sell the Hall.

As she turned to the door, she noticed a framed photograph on the wall. It was a picture of her grandparents in their youth, standing on the steps of the Hall. And behind them, central to the picture, stood the tall, slender figure of George Kendrake. He appeared to be hovering like a vulture over the innocent, youthful pair in front of him. It took all Ivory's willpower not to tear the photograph from the frame and destroy it. Her grandmother's words repeated in her head: "He pretended to be our friend, but all the time he was plotting to ruin your grandfather and take the Hall."

It was for her gentle grandfather's sake that Ivory wanted to discover exactly how the villainy had been perpetrated. John Meldrum's best friend had betrayed him, leaving him nothing, not even his pride.

And now another Meldrum had walked into the same trap, she thought with despair. She had come with vengeance in her heart, but Matthew had somehow made her quest seem less and less important. Why had she been fool enough to marry him?

She jumped and clutched at her throat as the phone rang from the Hall, its shrill ring echoing through the empty house. Wondering who could be calling when no one knew she was there, Ivory stared at the study door. The phone rang on and on, jangling along her nerves, until it occurred to her that the caller might be Matthew, with news of his return. She wrenched open the door and started out into the hall. But as she reached the phone, its ringing stopped.

Disappointment swept through her, and she realized how much she longed for the sound of his voice. She despaired of herself for wanting him so badly when she knew he was cold and unfeeling. But she knew that if he walked into the house at that moment, she would forgive him for everything.

The next morning, she breakfasted in the kitchen, missing Janey's bright inquisitiveness. Her stepdaughter ought to know she was home, so she decided to walk up to Top Farm to see the Garths before making a foray to the Home Farm, to the estate manager's office. It was possible that Angus Firth might have records going back for forty years.

It was a brisk, windy day with fluffy white clouds sailing across the sky. Alternate sunshine and shadow chased across the land. Ivory enjoyed her walk to the farm. It put color in her cheeks and made her eyes shine despite her restless night.

She was about to knock on the back door of Top Farm when Rob's voice said from behind her, "What are you doing back so soon?"

"My husband," Ivory said levelly, turning to face him, "was called away on urgent business, so I came home. Where's Janey?"

"Gone into town with Mum and Becky." He strolled toward her, the wind lifting a curly strand of fair hair as his glance took in her casual attire and her taut expression. "What's wrong, Ivory? Isn't it working out?"

"It's perfectly fine," she lied. "I'm annoyed that he rushed away, but then who wouldn't be? I expect it was some crisis they couldn't handle without him. My husband's quite a whiz kid, you know."

"Didn't he tell you what it was?" Rob asked.

"No. Actually I was asleep. A telegram came and he just left me a brief note. So I drove home alone yesterday."

"Oh, he did leave you the car?"

"Yes. Kind of him, wasn't it?"

Rob stuffed his hands into the pockets of his overalls, looking at her thoughtfully. "What did you marry him for, Ivory? I thought you must be in love with him, but I had doubts at the wedding. Has he got some hold on you?"

"I don't know what you mean," she snapped. The only "hold" Matthew had was one of the senses: a touch from him, even a glance from those blue eyes, could melt her. And of course there was Janey.

"You're not, er . . ." He looked her up and down, gauging the slenderness of her waist with speculative eyes.

Ivory's face flamed. "No, I'm not pregnant! What do you take me for? What's between him and me is our business, Rob. I only came to see Janey. I'll come back later and take her home. She might as well be with me."

"You know what Mum thinks, don't you?" Rob said.

"About what?"

"About your reasons for marrying Kendrake. She says you did it because he's rich and can give you all the things your grandmother made you feel you were entitled to."

Ivory's face paled with shock. Such a thought had never crossed her mind. Impulsively she laid a hand on Rob's arm. "You don't believe that, do you? Rob, it isn't like that. Oh, it's true he's able to give me material things, but I had quite a substantial legacy from my father, you know. I didn't marry Matthew just because—"

"Then why did you do it? Can you look me in the eye and tell me you love him?"

"I—I'm not sure," she said, unable to lie to him. "He's a complicated man, Rob. He's badly hurt and that makes him hard, at times. But I believe I can help him, if I try hard enough. And for Janey's sake . . ."

"Yes, I had a feeling it would be Janey," Rob said quietly. "I've always known there was a soft streak in you for motherless kids. It comes from being an orphan yourself. But it's no good reason for staying with a man you don't love." He laid his hands on her shoulders, pleading with her. "Leave him, Ivory. You can stay here until you decide what to do, but please don't stay with him any longer. You can't feel anything for a man like that. He's a human tiger. He'll eat you alive. I could see at that farce of a reception that you were afraid of him."

"I'm not!" she denied, startled that he could read her so accurately. "I can't just walk out. After a week? What would it do to Janey?"

"What will it do to you?" Rob returned.

She shrugged free of his hands and half turned away, holding a head that was suddenly throbbing. "It doesn't matter about me. Janey's the important one. To both of us. Rob—" Somehow she had to get him off this dangerous subject before she broke down and told him the truth, the shaming truth that she was sexually enslaved to a man she didn't even like, except the few times when she was allowed a glimpse behind his hard exterior. "Listen, Rob, I'm on my way to see Mr. Firth, the estate manager. You remember what happened forty years ago, how George Kendrake robbed my grandfather?"

Worriedly, Rob nodded. "I've heard the tale. What about it?"

"I'm going to see if I can find some concrete evidence to prove it. I feel I owe it to my grandparents to find out the truth. I'm not sure what I can do about it, but even so—"

"You must be mad!" Rob interrupted. "Why rake up ancient history? You wouldn't be able to do anything about it. What would you do, sue your own husband in the courts for something his uncle did? Take the Hall away from him?"

"I have a right to know the truth!" Ivory exclaimed. "Just to set the record straight, that's all. My grandmother was never clear about the details. I've got to know what really happened."

"And what do you expect to find, a signed confession? There won't be any evidence, Ivory. And if there was, what do you want to know for? So that you can tell your children—Kendrake children—about an old feud? Good grief, you're a Kendrake wife. You're mistress of the Hall. I'll bet your grandmother's jumping up and down with excitement. You've already set matters right, haven't you? You married George Kendrake's heir!"

Stunned, Ivory backed away. "Don't talk about my

grandmother that way! She was a wonderful woman.
She always did her best for me."

"She taught you to think yourself a cut above the rest
of us," Rob retorted. "She filled your head with her
own prejudices. Who knows what the truth really is?
You'd best leave it alone, Ivory."

She could hardly believe that Rob, her oldest and
dearest friend, had turned against her. Muttering something about coming back for Janey later, she swung
away and marched back up the track, the wind tossing
her pale hair.

Instead of making for Home Farm, she returned to
the Hall, her thoughts in turmoil. Rob's casual remark
about children—Kendrake children—had stupefied
her. It had never occurred to her there might be
children other than Janey. But suppose there were?
They would be Kendrakes, great-nieces and -nephews
of the nefarious George. Kendrake children: hers and
Matthew's.

Curled on the huge bed in the master suite, Ivory
found herself facing the reality of the situation into
which she had plunged herself. So far she had been
borne along by the memory of her grandmother's
teaching, but now it was as though a window had been
opened in her mind. There was no way of taking
revenge. George Kendrake was dead; her grandparents were dead. No action of hers could alter
their lives. Rob was right—even if she found proof,
what could she do but anger Matthew? Her quest
would drive the wedge deeper between them, when
in her heart she knew she wanted to close the gap,
not widen it.

Oh, Matthew. Matthew! She wrapped her arms
around the pillow and hugged it, wishing it had strong
arms, warm lips and blue-devil eyes. His uncle's crimes

were not his fault. He was hurt and bitter, but there were times when she glimpsed kindness and even tenderness in him. What she wanted most of all in the world was to persuade him to take down the barrier he had erected around his softer self. If only he would let her get close enough to try.

Chapter Nine

Ivory was out in the garden helping Rebecca and Janey set up the playhouse when Mrs. Barnes came rushing out, a smile wrinkling her whole face.

"He's home!" she exclaimed. "Mr. Kendrake's back. Taxi dropped him at the gate, so he said. He's gone up to his room—I mean, your room. Shall I do something special for dinner? Roast lamb, do you think?"

"Roast lamb will be fine," Ivory said standing up slowly. She was torn between jumping for joy and running away to hide somewhere. After almost three weeks away from Hedley-Magna, after deserting her on their honeymoon, how could he just walk in without warning? What on earth would she say to him? She went into the house and climbed the stairs, and went into the bedroom just as Matthew emerged from the dressing room, shirtless, a pair of cuff links in one hand.

At the sight of him, every nerve in Ivory's body was swamped by the reality of his presence. She forced herself to close the door and lean on it, then looked at him calmly.

Matthew's expression was guarded, too. "Do you have to live in those bloody trousers?" he said irritably. "You know I hate them."

"If you'd given me some warning—" Ivory began.

"Warning? You make it sound like an invasion. This happens to be my home, in case you'd forgotten."

Bitterness made her want to say that it was only his by default. But she closed her lips on the words and thought dismally that his absence had played its own tricks, making her forget how easily he could hurt her.

He strode across the room to drop the cuff links into a little leather box on the dresser. "Where's Janey?"

"In the garden, with Becky."

He looked round, his eyes narrowed. "Becky Garth? Have you been up to Top Farm?"

"Only when I collected Janey!" she exclaimed, annoyed by the hard suspicion in his voice. "I had to fetch her home, didn't I?"

"Yes, I suppose so. I need a shower. You keep an eye on those children. We don't want them falling into the pool."

Without answering, she slammed out of the room and ran down the stairs almost in tears. Marriage had evidently made little difference to her life.

Throughout dinner she was aware that his eyes devoured her, though he spoke mainly about the crisis that had called him away from the cottage on the moors. One of his close associates had died suddenly, obliging Matthew to spend time in London before flying to the States for consultations to ensure that the business ran smoothly.

"And wasn't there time to phone me?" Ivory asked acidly. "Did business keep you occupied twenty-four hours a day? Or did you just forget I might be worried?"

"If you'd been all that concerned, you could have contacted me," he said roughly.

"How could I, when I didn't know where you were?"

"I told you you could reach me through Harry Drummond, if you wished."

"When did you tell me that? I don't remember—"

"In the letter!"

"What letter?"

He glared at her, but the sight of her bewilderment took the edge off his temper. "Didn't you get it? Dammit, I posted it the minute I got to London. It should have reached you that Saturday at the latest. I know you were still at the cottage because I rang the Hall that Friday and Saturday evening and there was no reply."

"I . . . I was here," she confessed. "But the first night, by the time I reached the phone it had stopped ringing. And on Saturday you must have called while I was fetching Janey."

"And didn't Mrs. Wheeler forward the letter?" he demanded.

"I haven't seen any letter! There's been no word from you since that terse note you left at the cottage. I didn't know where you were, or why you'd gone, or how long you would be away."

"It was a misunderstanding, then." His lips were compressed as his blue eyes burned into hers. "I don't know about you, but I could do with an early night. You go up. I just want to make a phone call and find out what happened to that letter."

Ivory obeyed, but rebellion seethed inside her as she climbed the stairs. He had made no attempt to apologize, just ordered her to bed to wait for him, as if she were a concubine. Very well, if that was the way he wanted it, so be it.

She put on the seductive nightdress he had bought her. It left her arms and shoulders bare, and concealed very little of the rest of her. Turning out all but one lamp, which glowed in a corner, she sat in the big bed waiting for her husband to come and claim his marital rights.

He emerged from the dressing room wearing only a brown silk robe a shade darker than his skin. Even in the dim lighting she could see the desire that flared in his eyes at the sight of her.

"Mrs. Wheeler asked her son to post the letter on to you," he said. "He put it in his pocket and forgot about it."

"I see," she replied quietly, no longer interested in the letter.

Matthew stood before her with that thin robe clinging to his muscular shoulders, the front open to display a deep V of tanned chest. She had primed herself to remain cool as a doll in his arms, but just to look at him, tall and arrogant, his dark hair ruffled from undressing, worked strange emotions on her, making her realize how much she had missed him.

He sat down on the bed. His hand reached out to touch her shoulder and stroke the white length of her arm. Then his hand found hers, strong and brown against her pale fingers.

"That nightdress doesn't really suit you," he said gruffly. "The color's too dark. I ought to have bought white. Virginal white."

"It's a little late for that," she replied.

His eyes revealed that he, too, was remembering that time in front of the fire at the cottage, when she had given herself freely. His gaze rested on her mouth, making her lips ache for his kisses even while she steeled herself to be unresponsive.

"I owe you an apology," he said in a low voice. "I

meant what I said at the cottage. But I needn't have been so brutal about it.''

Before she could think of a reply, he pulled her into his arms, kissing her with a deep passion and tenderness that roared suddenly into desire. He slid down the straps of her nightdress, kissing her shoulders and her breasts, then her mouth again. His fingers explored her intimately, and when he lay beside her the urgency in his body assured her that there had been no other women to lighten his business trip. Ivory found herself giving kiss for kiss, caress for caress, caught up in the sensual wonder of him.

She woke the next morning to hear the shower rushing and Matthew whistling to himself, sounding full of life. He appeared wearing a bathrobe, rubbing his hair with a towel as he gave her a boyish grin. "Good morning, Mrs. Kendrake. Sleep well? I did, like a top." He leaned on his elbows either side of her, and his fingers caught in her hair as he dropped light kisses on her eyes, her nose, her cheeks.

The familiar sweet throb began in her veins. She could feel his warmth even through the bathrobe and the sheet, and her nostrils were full of the tangy aroma of the soap he used. When he was in this mood she could not deny him, or pretend she felt nothing for him. Her arms came up and locked round his neck, drawing his head down until his mouth was on hers, gently, moving with tender intent until she arched against him, silently demanding more of him.

Then Janey's voice sounded outside the door. Instantly Matthew rolled round to sit on the opposite side of the bed, while Ivory looked dazedly at the little curly-headed girl who rushed in beaming with delight.

"Aren't you ever going to get up?" Janey demanded.

"I've had my breakfast. Daddy, you promised we could go and buy me a new bike today. Oh, do hurry!"

"I believe I said after lunch," Matthew replied, easing himself to his feet as he wrapped the bathrobe more securely around him. "Scoot, Janey. Go and bother Mrs. Barnes."

Janey's face fell, her underlip thrusting out in the way it did when she was hurt and thinking of throwing a tantrum.

"No, it's all right, Janey," Ivory said swiftly, sitting up with the sheet protecting her. "Pass me my dressing gown, will you? You didn't tell me you were going to have a new bike."

"Daddy only said so last night when I was in bed," Janey replied, throwing a sullen look at her father as she handed Ivory the negligee. "Why do we have to wait until after lunch?"

"Because I've got things to do this morning," Matthew said. "Don't be so impatient."

As Ivory climbed from the bed one long shapely leg was displayed to her husband's interested eyes. Meeting his glance, feeling the glow still on her, she flushed and gave him a regretful look, to which he replied with a wry smile.

"I suppose you've been encouraging her to burst in here of a morning," he said drily. "I shall have to get a lock fixed. Maybe I'll buy one while we're in town. And something for you. What would you like, Mrs. Kendrake?"

You, she thought. I want you. But she said lightly, "I thought you valued me for my thrift."

"I do. Among other things." His gaze swept over her intimately, admiring the way her pale skin gleamed through the deep-blue silk. "My ivory maiden," he added under his breath.

The carpet was thick and soft under her bare feet as

she walked across to where he stood and looked up at him through her lashes, knowing how Eve had felt after she bit into the apple. "Hardly a maiden, not anymore," she murmured with a glance to where Janey was happily bouncing on the bed. "Anyway"—with a twinge of guilt she remembered the emerald pendant she had thrown into a drawer at the cottage on the moors—"you don't have to buy me anything."

"I feel like celebrating," Matthew said softly.

"Oh? Celebrating what?"

"The fact that I've given up some of my business responsibilities. Ah, I thought that would surprise you. I've resigned a couple of directorships, and I've appointed Harry Drummond as vice-chairman of Kendrake Enterprises, so if something comes up they won't need to keep running to me with their problems. Harry can do some of it. Which means that I can spend more time at home, now that I'm a married man with domestic commitments."

"You had those before," she reminded him with another glance at the oblivious child.

A shadow clouded his eyes, the lightness gone. "Yes, I know," he said, and turned away. "Go and get dressed, for heaven's sake, or I may forget we have an audience."

Ivory went into the bathroom. But as the water sprayed over her from the shower, she wondered why there was this barrier between Matthew and his daughter. Lately it had been less noticeable, so its reappearance struck her with renewed force.

It proved to be a happy day, one that Ivory was to look back on with nostalgia for a long time. After lunch they all drove into town and looked at bicycles, ordering a gleaming red one to be delivered the following day. Then Matthew insisted on buying Ivory a new dress to wear when he took her out to a celebration dinner that evening. She tried on a dozen before he was satisfied.

"I want to show you off," he said, looking askance at one daringly low-cut dress, "but not too much of you."

He was certainly possessive, but Ivory found herself glorying in it. He was more relaxed than she had ever seen him, seeming younger and more carefree. She was convinced that soon she would break right through his shell and rid him of his demon forever.

When they returned to the Hall, Matthew said that he needed to have a word with Angus Firth, the estate manager, and would walk up to Home Farm.

Getting ready for their dinner date, Ivory took a bath and washed her hair, then polished her nails. The new dress fit like a glove over her filmiest underwear.

When she was ready, Ivory decided to say good night to Janey, vaguely worried by the length of her husband's absence. He had been gone more than two hours, but presumably he had had a lot to discuss with Angus Firth.

She didn't hear him coming. The door opened and he was there. Ivory saw his grim expression in the mirror and swung round, alarmed. His frown was terrifying; his eyes glowed with contained fury in his dark face and the devil stared at her with open hostility.

"Matthew?" she breathed, a hand creeping to her throat.

"Making yourself beautiful?" he growled. "For me? How kind of you, Mrs. Kendrake. You do it really well, you know. All that creamy innocence. I'm lost in admiration for your guile."

"I don't know what you're talking about!" Ivory gasped.

"No? Then let me explain. Guess who I ran into in the lane: your old friend Rob Garth. Right by the cottage I've been having rebuilt because it was damaged by fire last year."

Her face went pale as she stood up, her thoughts in turmoil. What had Rob said to him?

"Ah, I see you understand me," Matthew said, his voice low and menacing. "It's strange, don't you think, that you've never thought to mention the fact that your grandparents were tenants of this estate? That you yourself were brought up not a hundred yards from where we're standing now?"

"I, I didn't think it was important," she faltered.

"Obviously you did, or you wouldn't have bothered to keep it secret. Did you think I was unaware of what the whole village thought of my uncle? They detested him, because their minds had been poisoned by a wicked old woman who—"

"She wasn't a wicked old woman!" Ivory broke in. "She was angry, justifiably angry, for her husband's sake. My grandfather was ruined by your uncle. He owned this Hall, and the estate, until his good friend George Kendrake tricked him out of them. This had been Meldrum land for ages."

His frown deepened, his eyes flashing blue sparks as he strode across the carpet and laid his hands round her pale throat, holding her so that she daren't move. "I could kill you, Ivory!" he said in a charged undertone. "You know that? I could snap your pretty little neck in two. You came here deliberately to humiliate me, didn't you? To get the last laugh on a Kendrake! Worming your way in here, getting at me through Janey. God, it was clever! Well, now you've got what you wanted. You're back at Hedley Hall, where you appear to think you belong."

Ivory flung up her hands to grasp his wrists, trying to free the grip on her shoulders. Fear and fury waged war inside her as she stared up at him with gray eyes almost eclipsed by the blackness of her pupils. "You won't hurt me, Matthew. Kendrakes don't act in the open. They plot and connive. Like your uncle plotted against my grandfather. If I've done the same, can you blame me?"

He released her as if her skin burned him. He swore at her, eloquently and obscenely, making Ivory wince at the crudity in his voice. Then he turned on his heel and went out, slamming the door behind him.

Closing her eyes against the well of hot tears, Ivory listened for some sound from Janey's room. If he had awakened the child . . . But the house remained silent. A short while later she heard the Mercedes' engine snarl as it sped away.

Sinking back onto the dressing stool, Ivory wept helplessly. Why had this had to happen now, when she and Matthew had almost reached an understanding? The day had been filled with joy, and now everything lay in ruins.

Eventually she calmed herself, washed her face and took off the new dress, deliberately substituting her oldest pair of jeans and a shapeless sweater. It was an act of defiance that made her feel better. When Matthew came back, she would show him she was no pretty plaything but a woman with a mind of her own. She would make him listen.

As she went down the stairs, the telephone rang. Mrs. Barnes came hurrying from the rear of the house.

"I'll get it," Ivory said.

The housekeeper looked worriedly at her mistress's swollen eyes and decided to hold her tongue, returning to her own territory.

"Hedley Hall," Ivory said into the mouthpiece.

"Ivory?" It was Corin Forsythe. "Is everything all right?"

"Everything is just dandy, thank you, Corin. Why?"

"Just wondered. There was a phone call a while ago. Carla went off to meet someone. She said she was seeing Matthew, but . . . She couldn't be, could she?"

Throwing a hand to her stinging eyes, Ivory leaned against the wall. "Is your sister given to lying?"

"She's not the most truthful person in the world, but . . . Look here, you sound a bit strained. Had a bit of a fight, have you? Do you want me to come round? After all, we never had a chance to finish what we started that night at the party."

"No, thank you, Corin," she said angrily. "In the future, I'd be grateful if you'd stay out of my affairs." She slammed the receiver down. No doubt she had offended him, but it didn't seem to matter.

If Matthew had gone straight to Carla's arms then nothing else mattered in the whole world.

Chapter Ten

She lay awake until the early hours and finally fell into a restless sleep, disturbed by nightmares in which nameless horrors kept separating her from her husband. When she awoke, she heard the shower running and leapt out of bed, seeing his clothes slung across the couch-bed in the dressing room. Had he just come in, after spending the night with Carla? Unaware that she looked haggard, Ivory waited unhappily for him to finish in the bathroom.

He came out wearing only a small towel draped round his waist. He looked at her, and without a word threw off the towel and began to dress as if she were not there. Ivory stretched out a shaking hand to touch his bare back, but he wrenched away from her, the blue devil in his eyes darting hatred at her.

"We can't go on like this," she said brokenly. "We've got to talk. It's true that my grandparents were the Meldrums. But I don't blame you for what your uncle did. Nor do I expect you to believe it, just on my word. Somewhere there'll be proof. If I could find it, and show you—"

Buttoning his shirt, he turned to face her grimly. "My uncle George was the kindest, most decent man I ever knew and I won't have you saying a word against him."

"Then he lived a lie!" Ivory cried. "He pretended to be a friend to my grandparents, but he managed to take everything they had, just because my grandmother chose someone other than him. If you'd had to live with them and watch a sick old man die slowly—"

"You'll have me crying in a minute," he said cynically. "I don't want to hear it. You got what you wanted: you're mistress of Hedley Hall. But you're also my wife. You married me of your own free will. And I intend to make sure you keep those vows you made. You owe me that. Think about it, Ivory. I'm going to be busy today. Just take care of Janey and stay out of my way."

"But we've got to—" she began, and stopped. She was talking to empty space.

He shut himself in the study, locked himself in and stayed there all day, except at lunchtime, when he came out and made himself pleasant to Janey. She was bubbling with delight over the new bicycle, which had been delivered that morning, and Rebecca was coming that afternoon to play. Janey's world was sunny, which was the only consolation Ivory had.

That evening, as she settled the child into bed and leaned to kiss her forehead, Matthew came in to say good night to his daughter. Ivory waited in the upstairs hall, anxious to see what he intended to do.

"Shall I fix you a drink before dinner?" she asked when he joined her.

He seemed remote, looking at her as if she were a stranger. "No, thank you. I'm eating out."

He strode on into the main bedroom, with Ivory at his heels demanding, "Where are you going? Out with

Carla again? I know you were with her last night. Corin took great pleasure in calling to tell me about it. If you think I'm going to put up with this, you're—"

"I shall see whomever I choose," he said brusquely. "I'm a Kendrake, remember? We do exactly as we please."

"Then go!" Ivory exclaimed. "Go to Carla. Go to the devil for all I care. I expect your uncle will be waiting for you."

The dressing room door closed in her face. Wanting to scream with impotent jealousy, she ran down to the drawing room and curled up on the settee. She heard him go out and the car purr away, crunching on the gravel. It was almost more than she could bear.

Alone in the dining room, Ivory picked at her meal, causing Mrs. Barnes to say, "You'll make yourself ill if you don't eat. You hardly had any of your lunch, either."

"I'm just not hungry." Wearily, she pushed her plate away. "Mrs. Barnes, would you mind watching Janey for an hour or so? I need a breath of fresh air."

"Yes, it'll do you good."

Ivory smiled wanly. Mrs. Barnes had guessed that something was wrong, but she was being very tactful about it. "Thank you. I don't know what we'd do without you, Mrs. Barnes."

The sun had just set, flinging its gold onto the underside of the dark clouds that lay across the western horizon. Hardly knowing where she was going, Ivory walked up the hill, pausing to look at the renovated cottage where she had once lived with her grandparents. Whatever Matthew might fondly believe about his uncle, Ivory knew her grandmother had told the truth. Lost in memories, she trudged on and her feet automatically turned along the lane toward Top Farm.

Rob looked stunned by the sight of her. "Ivory! You look awful. What's wrong? It's not Janey?"

"No, Rob." She managed a tired laugh. "Janey's fine. I just walked up to—to have a chat. I need to talk to someone."

Taking her arm, he led her inside the kitchen and put her into a chair. "Better sit down. Shall I make some tea?" He gestured to the books and papers strewn on the table. "I was just struggling with the accounts, so I'm glad of a break. Mum's gone out to a meeting."

"Good. I mean . . . It will be easier if she's not here. I know what she thinks of me. She wouldn't approve of my coming to cry on your shoulder."

"Is that what you've come for?" Rob asked softly.

She looked up, seeing his solid, dependable image waver through her tears. "Why did you have to tell Matthew I lived in that cottage? Do you know what you've done? He hates me now." Suddenly her misery spilled over and she laid her head on her arms, sobbing.

She felt Rob awkwardly stroking her hair. "Don't cry, Ivory," he said. "Please don't cry."

"But why did you tell him?"

"I thought he knew. I was just chatting—you know how you do. Honestly, Ivory, I didn't intend to make trouble. After what you said the last time you were here, I got to thinking. If that's the reason you married him, for revenge, then you must be out of your mind. It wouldn't have worked. Your husband has a right to know everything about you."

"Only if *I* choose to tell him!" She lifted her head, wondering how he could be so dense. But from the expression on his face she knew he had not foreseen the consequences of his innocent revelation. "He was furious. Couldn't you tell he was furious?"

Rob shook his head, propping himself on the table

beside her. "He went a bit quiet, but he kept asking questions. Then he thanked me and went off into the woods. Do you want a hanky?"

"I've got one, thank you." She pulled the handkerchief from her sleeve, still damp from earlier tears, and wiped her face dry.

"Vengeance never did anybody any good," Rob said sagely. "George Kendrake's dead, Ivory. You can't undo the past. I tried to tell you that the other day, but you wouldn't listen."

"Oh, Rob!" she sighed. "I did listen. You were right. I'd decided not to say anything, not ever. I knew it would ruin everything. And now it has. Don't you understand: by telling Matthew, you've spoiled every chance of our happiness. Or is that why you did it?"

Avoiding her eyes, he slid off the table and went to pour boiling water into the teapot. "You wouldn't have been happy, anyway."

"And that's why you did this?" Ivory breathed.

His shoulders slumped as he turned toward her. "I didn't think about it at the time. I'm not that clever. Honestly, I—I was just passing the time of day. I don't find it easy, talking to him. We've got nothing in common—except you. So it was a relief to find a subject he seemed to be interested in. It was only afterwards I wondered if . . . But it can't do any harm. It's not a real sort of marriage. It would be different if you were in love with him."

"Oh, but I am, Rob," she said sadly, a fresh tear running down her cheek. "I love him so much I can hardly bear it, and now he—he thinks I married him just to get the Hall back."

"Isn't that the truth?" he asked, setting the teapot on the table.

Ivory looked at her hands; they were pale and trembling, tearing at her handkerchief. "It was the excuse I gave myself, that, and Janey's security. But now I know that Matthew was my real reason. I've loved him from the start, from that very first day when I could see how vulnerable he was under all that toughness, when he tried so valiantly, so hopelessly, to handle Janey. I've been lying to myself all along. If only he would let me explain . . ."

"Well, give him a chance. His pride's been dented. But he won't stay angry with you for long. He'd have to be inhuman. Here, have some tea, and then I'll walk you home. If he's really what you want, I hope it all works out."

She ought to have been angry with him, she thought, but he just hadn't understood what he was doing. He had been hurt, too. By coming back to Hedley Magna she had caused nothing but harm, except for Janey. At least Janey still needed her. And Matthew . . . Matthew had gone to soothe his hurts in the willing arms of Carla Forsythe.

She and Rob walked back through the dusk to the side gate of the Hall almost opposite the cottage, where she turned impulsively in the shadows beneath the trees, bursting out, "Suppose he doesn't come home, Rob? If he stays out all night again, I—I just don't think I could bear it!"

"Hush, love." His arms came round her comfortingly, and she leaned on his broad chest as she might have leaned on a brother. "He'd be a fool to stay away when he's got you waiting for him. Where's he going to go, anyway?"

Somewhere with Carla Forsythe, she thought, biting her lip to stop the words from slipping out. Rob must never know about Matthew and Carla.

"He'll be home," he murmured soothingly, stroking her hair as he pressed her head to his shoulder.

A car swept over the hill, catching them full in its

headlights before it rushed past. Ivory pulled away from Rob, watching with thudding heart as the car slowed to turn in at the main gates on the corner below.

"It's Matthew!" she breathed. "Oh, Rob. If he saw us—"

"He must have," Rob said, shaking his head. "And unfortunately, there's no other woman around here with hair the color of yours. Lord, I'm sorry. I seem to have done nothing but complicate matters. Look, maybe I'd better come in with you and we'll explain to him together. I'll tell him you were upset and came to the farm to see Mum, like you used to do in the old days."

"That might not be such a good idea," she said dubiously.

"You forget I've seen him in a temper. I'm not leaving you to face him alone. No, don't argue. Come on."

He took her hand, and Ivory, feeling as though she had no will of her own and didn't care what happened, let him lead her through the gate and along the path.

There was no light on in the hall, but as she felt for the switch the lights blazed out, momentarily blinding her. As she blinked, she heard Matthew say tightly, "If you're coming to tell me you're leaving me, Ivory, you can save your breath. I'll never let you go."

"Oh, look here, Mr. Kendrake," Rob began. "It's not what—"

"Stay out of this!" Matthew snapped, striding to separate Ivory from the farmer, grabbing her arm and pulling her away. "She's my wife. She doesn't need you to protect her from me. Get out of here, Garth, or we'll both be sorry."

"I should never have let her marry you!" Rob exclaimed.

"As I remember," Matthew said coldly, "you

weren't given any say in the matter. It was none of your business then and it's even less your business now. Get out of here!"

Rob glanced at Ivory, about to say something, but then he thought better of it and departed. Ivory stood waiting, dismally certain that fate had chosen her as its plaything.

When Matthew turned his blue eyes on her, his contempt struck her like a physical blow. He had been drinking. She could smell the fumes from where she stood.

"I thought you'd gone out with Carla!" she flung at him.

"So you retaliate by running to your boyfriend?" he returned scornfully. "Or should I be more accurate and say your lover? You've been seeing him, haven't you?"

Her eyes grew huge in her white face. "Matthew, no!"

"Don't lie to me! I don't want to hear any more of your lies. God! I always swore it would never happen again, but I walked right into the same old trap. You're just like her—like Andrea. It's not just Rob Garth, is it? You've had Corin here while I was away. Or are you going to deny that, too?"

"Don't be ridiculous! He never—"

"I know what he's like," he cut in roughly, his eyes raking over her. "You weren't fighting him off at the party that night, were you? I thought you were different, Ivory. I really thought you were. Coming here all prim and proper. I even persuaded myself you weren't tempting me, but you were. That first day, when I found you in the pool, you knew exactly what you were doing. And that night, wearing that low-cut dress—you knew then you had me hooked, so you played the waiting game. It was all very clever."

"It wasn't deliberate!" she said desperately.

"That's what *she* said!" He caught her by the arms and swung her against the bannister, holding her there with hands like steel bands around her upper arms. She could smell the whisky strong on his breath, though he wasn't drunk. "She lied to me, too. But I'm not being made a fool of twice. You'll not see Rob Garth again, or Corin Forsythe, if I have to lock you up. You're my wife!"

"That doesn't make me your possession!" Ivory gasped. "You wouldn't dare lock me up in my own house."

His teeth bared in a snarl as he brought his face close to hers. "It isn't your house. It's mine. Mine to do with as I choose. Unless you do as I say, I shall sell it. There's been an American making inquiries about it."

"You can't! You wouldn't!"

With a wordless growl he released her and stepped back, a demonic light in his eyes. "That gets to you, doesn't it? You really care about this house. It's all you do care about, isn't it? For two pins I'd burn the place down. How would you like to watch it go up in flames?"

A wave of nausea made her sway, her sight clouding as she remembered all too vividly how her grandmother had died. She had been plagued by nightmares about fire for months afterwards. And now Matthew was threatening . . .

Sickly pallor robbed her face of all its color. As she crumpled, Matthew lunged forward to catch her in his arms. He lifted her bodily and climbed the stairs to the bedroom, gently laying her on the bed and bending over her anxiously.

"Ivory? Ivory!"

As she opened her eyes, his face swam into focus. For a moment she wondered where she was. Then the whole awful scene came back to her. She turned her face into the pillow, weeping.

There was silence in the room. She could feel his weight on the bed beside her and sensed his uncertainty, but she no longer cared. If he could believe that she would use her body to ensnare him, if he could believe that she would be unfaithful with two other men so soon after her marriage to him, then let him believe it. He had hurt her too much for her ever to forgive him.

Into the silence came Mrs. Barnes' voice, calling from somewhere along the corridor. "Janey? Janey, where are you?"

"Oh, God!" Matthew breathed, as if he too were at the end of his endurance. He left the bed and threw open the door. "What's wrong, Mrs. Barnes?"

"Oh, Mr. Kendrake," the housekeeper's voice came worriedly. "Janey's not in her room. I came to check because I looked out of my window just now and I thought I saw someone among the trees."

Still feeling dizzy, Ivory made her way to the door and saw Matthew check Janey's room. When he turned, his face was gray beneath its tan.

"You stay here," he ordered Ivory. "Mrs. Barnes, we'll search the house first. If we can't find her, you'll have to go up to Top Farm. She may have gone to find Becky Garth."

Mrs. Barnes ran down the stairs and began looking in all the rooms.

"Matthew," Ivory breathed in horror. "You don't think Janey heard us?"

"I think she very probably did," he said bitterly. "We should have thought of that before we started yelling at each other in the hall. Go and lie down. We'll find her. Don't worry."

It was all very well for him to tell her not to worry,

but as Ivory paced the bedroom she was imagining what their quarrel might have done to Janey. The little girl must have seen her world being shattered again, so she had run away, heaven only knew where.

Janey was not in the house. Unable to stay in the bedroom, Ivory went downstairs and saw Matthew set off into the woods while Mrs. Barnes dispatched her husband to Top Farm to alert the Garths. Ivory waited, her nerves in knots. She would never forgive herself if something had happened to Janey.

Mr. Barnes returned with the news that Rob was keeping a watch for the child.

"Should we tell the police?" Mrs. Barnes asked Ivory.

"No, not yet. Matthew may find her, or Rob might. She can't have gone far, can she?"

But Janey was eight years old, alone in the dark countryside, and unhappy. Silently, Ivory prayed that her stepdaughter might be found safe and well. The child had been through enough misery in her short life without being used by fate to punish her father and her new stepmother for their stupid adult quarrels.

When she heard the main door open, she rushed into the hall and stopped dead, gulping down her relief. Matthew had returned. In his arms was Janey, bedraggled and weary, her curly head drooping.

"She's all right," he said in a strangled voice. "Just worn out. She's been crying. Mrs. Barnes, will you warm some milk for her?"

He climbed the stairs. Beside him, Ivory peered at the tear-stained little face nestling into his shoulder. He laid Janey very gently on her bed, stroked her hair and leaned to press his lips to her forehead. Watching through her tears, Ivory thought with amazement, Why, he does love her! Why doesn't he let himself show it?

Janey lifted mournful wet eyes to look at Ivory, holding out her hand. When Ivory sat down on the bed opposite Matthew, the child threw cold arms around her neck.

"You won't leave me, Ivory, will you?" she sobbed. "Oh, please don't leave me!"

"I'll never leave you, Janey," Ivory promised, tears choking her own voice. "Never. Everything's all right."

Tucking the blankets round the child, she glanced at Matthew. Pain shot through her as she saw the anguish in his eyes. But he quickly blanked the expression and got up as Mrs. Barnes came in with the hot milk.

Ivory remained with her stepdaughter, talking quietly and singing lullabies. Gradually Janey calmed down, her eyelids drooping. But even after she was asleep Ivory remained on the bed, still crooning softly so that reassurance should creep into the little girl's dreams.

It was a chastened Ivory who eventually crept away, quietly closing the door of Janey's room before she trailed along to the master suite.

In the dim light she saw Matthew by the window staring out at the dark trees with smoke drifting from a thin cheroot between his fingers. He was still wearing slacks, but he had removed his shirt and put on his silk robe.

"I didn't know you smoked," she said quietly.

"I don't, as a rule," he replied. He turned toward her; the lamplight fell on smooth brown skin beneath the open robe. His face was somber, his eyes veiled by dark lashes. "We're to blame for what happened tonight, Ivory. I can't risk it happening again. Janey has a right to some real security."

"I know that. That's why I'm here."

His smile was cynical. "I almost believe it was partly for Janey that you married me. But it was the house, too. The only way the Meldrums could return to their ancestral home was by your marrying me. Isn't that the way your mind was running?"

"I'm too tired to have another argument, Matthew," she said with a sigh, making for the dressing room.

Out of his sight, she undressed and put on a cotton nightgown, removing her makeup before she returned to the bedroom. Matthew sat brooding in one of the low chairs by the window, the cheroot still trickling smoke toward the ceiling. He watched as she walked across the room and threw back the sheet to climb into the bed.

"Perhaps I should tell you the full truth about Janey," he said in a low voice, the glow from the lamp showing her the frown on his face.

"About her accident, you mean? Mrs. Barnes said—" She stopped herself, fearing that he might be angry if he knew the housekeeper had been gossiping.

He drew deeply on the cheroot and let the smoke trail from his nostrils as he squinted at her through it. "Well, go on. Mrs. Barnes said what?"

"That Janey had been in a motor accident, and her—her mother was killed."

"That's right." He stood up, tossing the end of the cheroot out of the open window, and walked to switch off the lamp. "But it started long before that. It started when I met Andrea."

Her eyes gradually became accustomed to the darkness. A streak of moonlight angled between the curtains, laying a square of paleness on the floor. Matthew walked through it, a tall, shadowy figure, and eased himself down to sit on the side of the bed.

"I was very young when I met Andrea." His voice came out of the shadows. "I loved her with all the tenderness and passion a young man can give his first love, even though I was only one of many. I dreamed of nothing else but making her mine, of sending away all the other men and having her all to myself."

The silence lengthened. Ivory was glad of the darkness, for she was sure her feelings must show on her face. If only he would love her like that!

"And?" she breathed.

He swung round, stretching out beside her with his arms folded behind his head, bringing the sharp but not unpleasant scent of smoke with him. "And then I was offered a chance to go to Australia, to be a partner in a sheep station. An old schoolfriend of mine was running it, but he needed more capital and extra help. So I got up the courage and gave Andrea an ultimatum: either she married me and came out to Australia, or I would do my best to forget I'd ever known her."

"And she accepted?" Ivory managed.

"No." A sharp laugh escaped him and she heard the pain in it. "No, she turned me down flat. So I went out to Wallaroola station and threw myself into the work, determined to get her out of my system. It wasn't easy, but after a year I'd nearly managed it. That's when she came. She just arrived, without warning. She threw herself at me and wept and said she'd missed me and would I have her back. Would I? Like a shot, poor bloody fool that I was. We were married. And that was when the dream turned sour. I realized I'd never really known her. And after about a week she told me. She'd only married me to get back at some other man who'd jilted her. She never wanted me. She never wanted to live in Australia. She hated the place. She even hated me touching her. So we moved into separate rooms."

He stirred restlessly, turning on his side towards her as he leaned on one elbow. "She had started making arrangements to leave when she found out she was pregnant. You can imagine the quarrels that followed.

She thought I'd trapped her. She said I'd ruined her life. She hated and despised me, she hated the child inside her. She even went for long rides in the heat, galloping for miles, to try and get rid of . . . God!" He sat up suddenly, turning his back on her, his head in his hands.

"Matthew, don't!" she begged, moving to wrap her arms around his broad shoulders.

He shook her off roughly, wrenched himself to his feet and went to lean on the window frame. "I won't try to describe the few months that followed. Janey was born, eventually, and a few days later Andrea walked out. She said she needed her friends and some social life. She needed men around her, that's what she meant. At Wallaroola there was only me and my partner, and he was solidly married, with four kids. Andrea always craved attention from a dozen men at a time."

"But do you mean she left on her own?" Ivory asked incredulously. "She abandoned Janey?"

"A baby would have gotten in her way. Anyway, Janey was better off at Wallaroola station rather than leading the sort of life I heard Andrea was leading, flitting from one man to the next."

"Then why didn't you divorce her?"

He swung round, the lines of his face made harder by the moonlight, all angles and shadowy planes. "Because as far as I'm concerned when I say 'Till death do us part' I mean it. Besides, she never applied for a divorce. It didn't matter to her whether she was married or not. She was perfectly happy the way things were, until—" He broke off and with a muffled exclamation slammed his fist against the window frame.

"Until eighteen months ago," he went on tiredly. "Soon after my uncle died, in fact. I expect Andrea heard I'd come into money. I had to come over here to sort out the legal side, so I left Janey in the care of my partner's wife. When eventually I did get back, Janey had gone. Only a few days before, Andrea had flown in with some man in his plane, and while my partner's wife was busy making coffee, they snatched Janey."

Scrambling off the bed, Ivory ran to his side and laid a hand on his arm. "Oh, Matthew, no!"

"Of course I alerted the authorities," he said, too intent on his story to take notice of her, "but by then Andrea and Janey had vanished. There was no news of them. None of Andrea's friends in England knew where they were, though there was talk of some new boyfriend she was living with in the West country. I followed several false trails. Then last October Andrea contacted me. She offered to return Janey if I would pay her enough money to set her up in business. But before I could do anything, the accident happened. There was a car crash. Andrea and her current lover were killed, and Janey . . . Janey was injured quite badly."

Not knowing what to say, Ivory rubbed her cheek on his sleeve, and felt him move away.

"The worst of it was what it had done to Janey's mind," he went on. "At first she wouldn't have me near her. She seemed to blame me for everything. Gradually I realized that Andrea had poisoned her mind against me. She was so disturbed that they kept her under observation for months, and when they said I could bring her home I wanted to get her right away from everything that might remind her of Andrea. So I brought her here."

"I didn't understand," she said sadly, caressing the warm silk of his sleeve. "You've been afraid of losing her again, haven't you? I wish you had told me before."

He jerked away as if he couldn't bear her touch, swinging round to look at her with a face made craggy by moonlight. "Told you what? That I'm a fool who can be taken in by a woman's lies? But you know that, don't you? It's happened again. First Andrea, and now you, you with your false innocence and your vengeful heart. I warn you, Ivory, if you cause Janey any more hurt, you'll wish you'd never been born!"

"You don't have to tell me that!" she breathed. "I'd never hurt her, Matthew."

"You'd better mean that," he growled. "Because that's all I want from you. That, and—"

His hands clamped on her shoulders, pulling her roughly against him. His arms came round her, molding her against his body. One hand in her hair jerked her head back, and as she cried out, the sound was smothered by his mouth.

She struggled impotently against his greater strength, pushed her hands between them to force him away. But her fingers encountered smooth warm flesh, and she felt the familiar heat rise in her, a sweet languor that made her stop resisting. Hot tears welled in her eyes.

He bent and tossed her up into his arms as if she were Janey's size, her pale hair trailing across his dark robe as she leaned her head on his shoulder.

"Matthew, don't," she begged. "Not like this."

"Then how?" he muttered, laying her across the bed. "Show me how."

"You know how!" Ivory groaned.

He did know. Slowly and skilfully, he removed her nightdress, touching every inch of her skin as it was uncovered, warm lips following a path traced by his fingers until she trembled helplessly, bewitched by the spell only he could weave on her.

"Like this?" he murmured, his mouth making her breasts ache with desire as he kissed them and let his tongue flick her skin. "Like this?"

Her nails caught across his back, up his spine and

into his hair. She pulled his head up to kiss his mouth, feeling his body naked against hers, his need evident.

"I love you," she whispered into the darkness. "Matthew, I love you."

"You mean you want me," he amended harshly, his breath warm on her ear. "Say that. Say it!"

"I want you," she breathed despairingly. "Oh, I want you."

"That's better. That's the truth."

This time he was in no hurry. He worked on her until she cried out with desire and lifted herself against him, her whole being craving fulfillment. He lifted her to the stars and she saw them explode around her, aware that he had reached the same peak of ecstasy at the same moment.

She tasted salt and knew it was from her own tears. He made love like a master of the art, but for her it was more than physical. How could she make him believe that she loved him? He had been badly wounded by one lying woman; now he thought her a liar, too. He would never trust her again.

And the worst of it was that he had good reason. She hadn't lied, but she had deliberately misled him about her origins. It had all seemed so simple and so just—until she fell in love with the man who was supposed to be the enemy.

Chapter Eleven

She woke early, disturbed by a dream about Janey, and found Matthew asleep beside her, one arm thrown possessively about her waist. He looked touchingly youthful, the stern lines wiped from his face, the dark lashes sweeping down toward his brown cheeks. His mouth looked different, too, in a vulnerable curve that made her want to kiss him into wakefulness.

Very gently, she lifted his arm and slipped out of bed. He stirred, turned over, but seemed to settle back into sleep. Ivory threw on a light kimono and silently left the room, hurrying barefoot along the passage to open Janey's door softly.

Janey was awake, sitting up in bed reading to herself, her lips moving as her finger followed the words across the page. She looked at Ivory uncertainly, her eyes big as a calf's and liquid with mute questions.

"How are you feeling?" Ivory asked, sitting beside her.

"I had a nightmare," Janey said. "I thought you were going to go away and leave me."

Hiding her tears, Ivory hugged the child, ruffling the

brown curls. "You know I wouldn't do that, Janey. I love you too much ever to leave you. You're my little girl now. And I've been thinking: how would you like to go to real school, after the holidays?"

Janey looked up, her eyes full of hope. "On the bus with Becky? Every day? And—and come home at night? Not a boarding school?"

"Of course not a boarding school!" Ivory said with a shaky laugh. "Your daddy and I would miss you too much if we didn't see you every day. But it would be nice to go to school with other children, wouldn't it? You'll make lots of friends, and you can bring them home. And on your birthday we'll have a party. When is your birthday?"

"In October. Can we really, Ivory? Have a real party?"

"A real party. A cake with candles, and games with prizes, and balloons."

Janey leapt up in bed to throw her arms round Ivory's neck. "I do love you, Ivory."

"And I love you," Ivory said, warmed by affection so freely given.

Drawing away, Janey looked at her with sudden doubt clouding her eyes. "Do you love Daddy, too?"

Ivory took a breath, guessing that Matthew's first wife had told Janey she hated him, probably trying to make Janey hate him, too. As if it hadn't been enough to make use of him and then throw his love back in his face, Andrea had taken it upon herself to turn Janey against her father.

"Yes, Janey," she said quietly, speaking from her heart. "I love your daddy very much."

"He does want me, doesn't he?" Janey asked wistfully. "I mean, when he gets mad at me—"

"Well, he gets mad at me, too, sometimes, doesn't he? People do, you know. And you've got quite a temper yourself, young lady. But just because we have arguments, it doesn't mean we don't love each other, now does it?"

"I suppose not," Janey said, her face clearing. "Then everything's all right?"

"Everything's just fine. Now I must go and get dressed, and you'd better have your wash."

As she closed the door she saw her husband leaning in the doorway of the master suite wearing his bathrobe, hair tousled and his blue eyes gleaming with derision.

"You should have been an actress," he sneered as she approached him. "Still, if you can convince Janey to stay happy, I suppose I shouldn't complain."

"You heard?" Ivory said softly, staring at him, her wide, hurt eyes as gray as morning mist.

"Most of it. I was anxious about her, too, but you seemed to be coping admirably. I didn't want to break in on your most important scene."

Stung, she said sharply, "I wasn't acting!"

"No? I would be careful, if I were you. All those Meldrum ancestors turning in their graves. You'll betray them all and they'll come to haunt you."

"I don't care about that anymore! What I said to Janey is true, even if you don't believe me. Someday I'll make you believe me."

One eyebrow rose in a way that infuriated her. "Andrea tried that," he said. "She succeeded, which is why I'm sure it won't happen again. Excuse me."

Turning away, he strode to the bathroom and locked himself in.

The day continued in the same vein, with Matthew incarcerated in the study. He didn't even come out for lunch, but had Mrs. Barnes take a tray in for him. Ivory could only be thankful that Janey had convinced herself the previous night's episode must have been a bad dream.

Since the weather was cool and showery, they had spent the morning doing lessons. Janey's reading was improving slowly, but she refused to concentrate for very long and kept rushing to the window, expecting Becky Garth to arrive. After lunch she grew restless, asking where Becky could be; she had promised to come and bring her pony.

Ivory invented excuses for Becky, though she thought that the girl had probably been told not to come to the Hall again, not after the way Matthew had spoken to Rob. The gap between Ivory and her old friends seemed to widen with every encounter.

There also remained the gulf between Ivory and her husband. Although he was in the house, for all the communication there was between them he might as well have been a hundred miles away. And it was all because of George Kendrake. It seemed to Ivory that the only way to amend matters was for her to find a way to prove that George Kendrake had been less than a paragon. Then she could go to Matthew and say, "Look, it is true. My grandmother was justified in what she said and I did have good reason to be angry. But it doesn't matter to us. It's all in the past. Please can we forget about it? Can we start afresh?"

Eventually, leaving Janey in the playroom, Ivory went down to the kitchen to find Mrs. Barnes, feeling in need of some adult conversation. The housekeeper was busy baking, damp cloths covering bowls of rising bread while she beat eggs into softened butter for a cake.

They talked about cooking, and somehow the conversation turned to those weekend parties George Kendrake had been fond of giving. Mrs. Barnes and her

husband had come to work for him only about a year
before his death, but she had tales in plenty about the
catering problems his visitors had brought.

"I seem to remember Mrs. Mead was housekeeper
here before you," Ivory said. "She was a strange old
soul. She really kept to herself. She wouldn't talk to the
villagers."

"She didn't like their attitude to Sir George," Mrs.
Barnes said. "I never did hear the full tale, but he was
supposed to have done something awful in his youth. I
expect you heard about that, too, with you knowing the
Garths. Personally, I don't believe in listening to
gossip. I exchange the time of day if I meet people
about the village, and I've had one or two chats with
Mrs. Garth, but I've come across this queer sort of
hostility myself, so I generally keep clear of people.
I've got enough to do here. Anyway, I work for the
Kendrakes, and they've been good to me."

Ivory was wryly amused by the pronouncement
about gossip. It was Mrs. Barnes' own indiscretion that
had brought her there in the first place.

"Did Mrs. Mead work here for long?" she asked.

"Donkeys' years," the housekeeper said. "Since she
was a girl, I believe. Started out as a housemaid. Before
the war, that must have been, when the previous
owners lived here. The Meldrums. There was still a
Mrs. Meldrum living in the village when we came, but
she died in a fire, poor soul."

"I know," Ivory said quietly. "She was my grandmother."

Mrs. Barnes stopped beating and gaped at her.
"Your grandmother? Oh, I'm sorry. I didn't know."

"I'm aware of that. It doesn't matter. But since
you're almost bound to hear it sooner or later, I
thought I'd tell you myself. Is Mrs. Mead still alive, do
you know? Does she live nearby?"

"Why, yes." She still looked dazed and took a moment to collect her thoughts. "Sir George pensioned her off. She lives in the cottage in Holly Wood. It's a queer old place, and she's practically a recluse, living with her cats. I go over there occasionally to buy a jar of honey; the old girl keeps bees, you see. But I like to make sure she's all right, too. Why do you ask?"

Ivory shrugged casually. "Just curious. Besides, if she's a pensioner on the estate, I ought to take an interest. Do we need any honey at the moment? Perhaps I could go and visit her and introduce myself."

"Well, yes, as a matter of fact I could do with a couple more jars. Young Janey loves toast and honey for her tea. If you're sure it's no trouble."

Ivory changed into sturdy shoes, slipped on a raincoat and set out to walk to Holly Wood. It lay behind the church, reached via a pathway edged with tall weeds that dripped as she brushed past.

The cottage was set in a clearing, a low, thatched building with its roof coming down like shaggy brows over leaded windows. Its garden was bright with summer flowers, alive with the hum of dozens of bees. As Ivory clicked the gate shut behind her, a dumpy figure wearing a wide-brimmed hat shrouded with netting appeared round the corner of the cottage with a smoke-gun in one hand drifting white trailers.

"What do you want?" the figure demanded gruffly.

"I've come to buy some honey," Ivory said. "And to introduce myself. I'm Mrs. Matthew Kendrake, from the Hall. Are you Mrs. Mead?"

The sound of the name Kendrake worked magic. The old lady threw back the veil of her hat and surveyed Ivory with twinkling eyes in a kindly, rosy face. "Well, I never! I heard there'd been a wedding. How kind of you to come. Come in, Mrs. Kendrake. Come in."

The cottage was tiny and seemed to be full of cats.

They padded, stretched and slept on every available surface. Mrs. Mead shooed one off an overstuffed armchair and invited Ivory to sit down while she made a pot of tea.

"I don't often get visitors," she said. "I don't much care to associate with the folk of Hedley Magna. Most of them avoid me, anyway. They think I'm a witch." Her false teeth clicked as she grinned broadly. "Maybe I am."

Looking around the cottage, which was hung with drying herbs and decorated with copper pots, Ivory could understand the feeling. She accepted a cup of herb tea and exchanged small talk for a while, trying to bring the conversation round to George Kendrake. Mrs. Mead probably knew something of what had happened forty years before, since she had been at Hedley Hall when the transfer from Meldrums to Kendrakes took place.

But when she eventually mentioned the name of George Kendrake, the old lady peered at her narrowly from her chair by the table.

"I've seen you before somewhere. From the village, aren't you?"

"I was brought up in Hedley Magna," Ivory confessed.

"I thought so. Why—aren't you Anna Meldrum's granddaughter? Of course, that's it! I knew your face was familiar. Well, isn't that strange. A Meldrum come back to the Hall after all these years."

"Yes," Ivory said, deciding that the best course was total honesty. "And it's causing trouble between me and my husband. He swears his uncle George was the finest man who ever walked the earth, but I know he was a cheat and deceiver."

Instantly, the old lady's mouth pinched. "That he was not!"

"But he was! My grandmother told me—"

"She told you what she thought was the truth. I can't blame her for that. And she was loyal to her husband. But I saw it happen. I know what went on. I wasn't averse to a bit of eavesdropping in my younger days, and I heard more than most."

"But it is a fact that George Kendrake took the estate from my grandfather," Ivory said obstinately.

Mrs. Mead sighed, folding her twisted hands in her lap. "It's a fact that he bought it, but he did that to save your grandfather, not to ruin him. John Meldrum—ah, he was a fine young man, handsome as they come. But he was reckless. He had no sense where money was concerned. He used to gamble. I often heard George Kendrake warning him against it, but he wouldn't listen.

"Then there was Anna, your grandmother. They both loved her, but she chose John Meldrum, not knowing what he was like. He was a weak man, always looking for the easy way out, always blaming other people for his faults."

"That's not true!" Ivory exclaimed.

"Ah, my dear," the old lady said sadly, "I've got no call to lie to you. Whatever you've been told, the truth is that George Kendrake stayed around because he could see which way things were heading. He wanted to save Anna from poverty. He never stopped loving her. That's the plain truth. Even though she'd married another man, he went on loving her. And he did all he could to help John Meldrum.

"All the time, your grandfather was getting deeper and deeper into debt, borrowing money here, there and everywhere to keep up appearances, so that Anna wouldn't know what was going on. He kept gambling, hoping to win back his fortune, but of course it only made things worse. Finally he had nothing left. It would have meant bankruptcy and probably prison if George Kendrake hadn't bought the estate, to cover the debts. To save Anna from disgrace, don't you see?"

"But it was his bad advice that made my grandfather penniless!" Ivory protested.

Mrs. Mead shook her head. "That's what your grandfather told your grandmother. He blamed it all on George Kendrake. It was easier than confessing to his own stupidity. I think even Anna had her doubts, but she was loyal to her husband. Over the years, to protect him, she built up the tale of how George Kendrake had robbed them, until I think she believed every word of it herself. But your grandfather knew the truth. He had to live with that lie. That's what made him ill. That's what killed him, in the end. He just couldn't admit that he'd been a wastrel and a failure."

Ivory was silent, looking down into her cup. It was not easy to accept this new version of the story. But Mrs. Mead had been a disinterested observer, and what she said did fit all the facts as Ivory knew them. Her grandmother had always been overprotective of her grandfather, defending him against all comers. If she had sensed the truth, she had refused to believe it. And she had made sure that Ivory herself never suspected. It explained why John Meldrum had led his wife to believe he owned the cottage where they had lived: it let him keep a little of his pride. And all the time George Kendrake had been their savior, not their enemy. How hurt he must have been when he heard what his beloved Anna was saying about him.

She left the cottage carrying two pots of Mrs. Mead's golden honey, sadness clouding her gray eyes. She, too, had believed the tale and had let it spoil her relationship with Matthew. It would be too stupid if they spent their lives, as her grandparents had done, not being honest with one another. But if she went to him and apologized, would he believe her?

Dismally she thought that nothing would make him love her. He must think she was a liar—which was probably what he thought of her grandmother. He probably thought that lying came easily to all Meldrums. Well, hadn't she thought that all Kendrakes were cold and ruthless? It was hopeless. Hopeless!

"Ivory?" Rob's voice made her stop and look up. He stood on the path, a shotgun in one hand. "What are you doing here? Oh, been to see the old witch, have you? Her bees do make marvelous honey."

"So Mrs. Barnes told me. Rob, I can't stop now. I must get home."

"Everything's all right, is it?" he asked. "Becky wanted to come over today, but I told her she'd better stay clear for a while. Was he very angry?"

"Yes, he was—as he had every right to be. I should never have come running to you."

He smiled wryly at her. "As long as it's all over now. Is Janey okay? What made her run away?"

"Oh, a misunderstanding, that's all. She's fine today."

"I'm glad. By the way, do you remember Maggie Randall? She helps her parents run the post office. I'm taking her to a dance on the weekend."

"I hope you have a lovely time," she replied, meaning it. "But I must go. Excuse me."

To pass him, she had to step into the wet grass. Her heel caught on a hidden stick, overbalancing her. Trying to save the honey, she stumbled awkwardly to her knees, her hat flying into the undergrowth.

"Steady!" Rob caught her arm, helping her up. "You all right? Wait, I'll get your hat."

He rescued it, then carefully settled it on her head,

giving her a rueful smile. "You look about sixteen in that outfit. Remember how I used to mooch about in the lane hoping you'd come out for a walk?"

"Yes, I remember." She rubbed her bruised knee, clutching the jars of honey to her, the distress clear in her eyes. "Rob, please excuse me. I want to get back to the Hall."

"Back to your husband," he said with a sad little smile, stepping forward to brush his lips across her cheek. "Good-bye, Mrs. Kendrake. I have to get on myself. Be seeing you."

He turned away and disappeared into the shadows of the wood. For a moment Ivory watched him, aware that the final ties with the old life had been broken by that visit to Mrs. Mead. The past was unimportant. Even Rob was part of the past now, and if he had started seeing someone else, then she need no longer feel guilty about him. She must think only of the future, which meant building a real life with Matthew and Janey.

As she walked along the path by the church, she was dismayed to see the Mercedes, with Matthew at the wheel, sweep out of the drive from the Hall and turn up the lane. She held the jars of honey in one arm, waving the other as she ran out into the road, calling, "Matthew! Matthew, wait!"

He must have seen her in the rear-view mirror. But the car snarled up through the gears and was gone, up the hill past the old Meldrum cottage and over the brow. Despairing, Ivory trudged back to the house.

"Did my husband say where he was going?" she asked of Mrs. Barnes, who was just taking her cakes out of the oven, golden brown and smelling delicious. "I saw the car leaving."

The housekeeper set the hot pans on a grid, her tongue caught between her teeth in concentration.

"Didn't he find you, then? Well, I can't understand that. He knows where Mrs. Mead lives. That is a shame. I'm afraid he's been called away again, to London. He packed and then went to find you, to tell you about it, but a few minutes later he was back. He just threw his things into the car and went off. Must have been in a hurry."

"Yes, it seems like it."

She went upstairs to take off her raincoat and sat on the end of the big bed with her head in her hands. Matthew had gone—again—after promising to spend more time at home. Just when she had wanted to talk to him seriously. It was so unfair. If he had set out to find her, then why . . .

A heavy sigh escaped her. Had Matthew seen her with Rob? Oh, no!

Despairingly she stared at the thick brown carpet, arguing with herself. Matthew was impossible. He had gone off to Carla only two nights before, hadn't he? He didn't expect her to object to that. But she wasn't even allowed to speak to an old friend. When he came back, she must make him see that they couldn't live like this. Marriage needed trust on both sides.

But Matthew did not come home. Nor was there any word from him.

After two days, Ivory looked up the Drummonds' number, and discovered from Nancy that Matthew was staying at a hotel in the city. She phoned that evening, only to be told that Mr. Kendrake was out. She tried again the next day, with the same result, so she left a message for Matthew to call her when he came in. She suspected he had told the hotel switchboard always to say he was out if his wife called. If he was deliberately preventing her from contacting him, then what was she supposed to do? Or was he going out every evening, in company with some attractive female?

The month of August drifted by amid sunshine and showers. Toward the end of the month Ivory woke feeling ill, as she had done several mornings. She had not been eating well and Matthew's continued silence depressed her. It was no wonder she felt ill at times.

Then Janey rushed in, waving a letter. "It's from Daddy!" she cried, leaping onto the bed.

Ivory took the letter with a wave of hope and relief. "Darling, please don't bounce on the bed. Why don't you go and have your breakfast? I'll tell you what Daddy says later."

"Okay," Janey agreed, and skipped out in the highest spirits.

Tearing the envelope with overeager hands, Ivory saw the black, definite handwriting slanting across the page. It filled her with joy, until she read the message:

"My dear Ivory, I have now had time to think things through and have decided that the best thing for us all would be for me to return to Australia. Janey will be happiest with you. You may stay at the Hall, which is what you wanted, I believe. As you know, I do not believe in divorce, but after a certain amount of time the law will allow you to break the ties without my cooperation, as you probably know. I believe it's five years. You're young enough to wait and doubtless Rob Garth will be around to keep you company.

For myself, two disastrous marriages have convinced me I shall never wish to take the risk again. I shall probably be in London from time to time on business, should you wish to contact me through the Drummonds. I shall make all necessary arrangements regarding finance, etc. You may safely leave the running of the estate to

Angus Firth. All I ask is that you take good care
of Janey.

Matthew

Ivory stared at the letter. The jagged writing blurred
through her tears. How cold and efficient it sounded.
He had decided. Didn't she have any choice in the
matter?

Suddenly her stomach churned and she ran for the
bathroom, doubled up with nausea. He couldn't do this
to her. He couldn't!

This time it was Ivory who shut herself in the study,
using Matthew's spare keys since she now knew where
he kept them. Fumbling in her haste, still feeling
queasy, she found a file relating to Kendrake Enterprises and the phone number.

Her fingers shook as she turned the dial and heard it
ring. There was a click and a female voice said,
"Kendrake Enterprises."

"I'd like to speak to Mr. Kendrake, please," Ivory
said.

"Who's calling?" the voice asked.

"It's Mrs. Kendrake. His wife."

The voice told her to wait one moment. Ivory sat
hunched in the swivel chair, wondering exactly what
she was going to say, but yet another woman's voice
came through, low and sexy.

"Mrs. Kendrake? This is Sheila Farrell. I'm afraid
your husband's in a meeting. I can't possibly interrupt
him at the moment. May I take a message?"

"No. No, thank you. I'll try again later." She put the
phone down, her head aching with unshed tears as she
wondered what the owner of that husky contralto
looked like. Her imagination conjured images of a
willowy brunette to match the voice. She ought to have

known that the way to Matthew would be barred by receptionists and secretaries, at least during office hours. And after?

But this time she wasn't going to let herself be blocked; it was too important. She dialed the Drummonds' number. A few moments later, Nancy Drummond answered her.

"Nancy!" Ivory said hurriedly. "This is Ivory Kendrake again. I'm trying to reach Matthew but he's in a meeting or something. I haven't been able to reach him at the hotel, either, and—"

"Oh, he's moved out of that hotel," Nancy said. "He's staying with us. It seemed crazy for him to be all alone when we've got ample room here. Ivory, is there something wrong between you two? Forgive me for asking, but he's been so tense lately, and now this talk of going back to Australia—"

"That's what I want to see him about," Ivory replied. "Nancy, I know it's an imposition, but would you mind if I came down for a couple of days? I've got to talk to Matthew and I can't do it over the phone."

"You'd be welcome. Yes, do come. I've a feeling you're the only one who can snap him out of this black mood he's got himself into. And we're fond of him, you know."

Ivory took note of the address, thanked Nancy, and rang off. Going to London herself, to make Matthew listen to her, was the only course she had left. If it didn't work . . . But she mustn't be defeatist. It had to work.

She told Janey and Mrs. Barnes that she was going to join Matthew for a few days and hoped to bring him back with her.

Throwing some clothes into a case, she set off. "Good luck," had been Mrs. Barnes' farewell to her, and Ivory knew the housekeeper sensed that something was badly amiss.

Not bothering to stop for a meal, she drove through the outskirts of London and on into the lovely county of Kent. The Drummonds lived in a little village not far from Maidstone, in what proved to be a large modern house built on a hillside and fronted by sloping lawns and shrubberies.

"You look dreadful," Nancy Drummond said frankly, greeting her at the door. "I wasn't expecting you for ages yet. You must have driven straight through. No lunch?"

"No. Not much breakfast, either. Nancy, what time do you expect Matthew back?"

"Not before seven. Maybe later, if this board meeting is as complicated as they were expecting. You'll have time to get freshened up and have a rest. You look as though you need it. Tell you what, you get settled in and I'll fix you a sandwich and a nice cup of tea. And take your time, Ivory. You don't look at all well."

She installed Ivory in the room Matthew was using, a guest room with its own bathroom. Ivory was comforted by the sight of her husband's belongings. But the mirror told her why her hostess was so concerned about her: her face was pale as death, with deep circles caused by strain lying under her eyes.

She took a cool shower and some aspirin for her headache, then put on a light cotton dress and went downstairs.

"Better?" Nancy inquired, pouring tea at a low glass table on which stood a plate of sandwiches.

"Much better, thank you. I only hope I'm doing the right thing. He might be annoyed that I've come."

"He'll be worried that you nearly killed yourself getting here, but he'll be glad to see you. I'm not going to ask what's wrong, Ivory, but I do know that Matthew's been miserable ever since he left Hedley Magna. Last time he was here—when he had to desert you on your honeymoon—he talked of nothing else but you. He kept showing everybody that picture he's got."

"Picture?" Ivory said blankly.

"That sketch he's done. Haven't you seen it? It's a very good likeness, though he kept saying it doesn't do you justice. I expect you know he loves you a great deal, more than he's prepared to admit, probably. He's not one to wear his heart on his sleeve."

Relaxing against the cushions, Ivory nibbled a sandwich and thought that her husband's heart was securely locked up and the key had been thrown away. But it was strange that he should have a sketch of her. Of course she had seen him scribbling on occasion, but she had always thought he was making business notes.

"Have you told him I was coming?" she asked.

"On a board-meeting day?" Nancy laughed. "My dear girl, when the board is in discussion nobody, but nobody, can get in touch with them, short of a real crisis. That dragon Miss Farrell sees to that."

"She didn't sound like a dragon over the phone," Ivory said dubiously. "I suppose she's beautiful and sophisticated—"

"What, Sheila Farrell? She's fifty if she's a day. But she's very efficient. Harry often says he doesn't know what they'd do without Miss Farrell. What have you been thinking, that Matthew was spending his time with other women? Oh, really! He hasn't looked at another woman since he met you. He's not the womanizing type."

"What about Carla Forsythe?"

"What about her? I can assure you, she's the one who did all the running. Do you know, she even flew out to Australia to corner him there a couple of years ago?"

"I heard he invited her," Ivory said.

Nancy snorted. "Then your information's wrong. He's spent most of his time trying to avoid her. He eventually got rid of her by telling her he'd never divorce Andrea. And then there was all that trouble over Janey. Andrea kidnapped her. I expect you know about that."

"Yes, I do."

"He came over here nearly out of his mind with worry," Nancy told her. "And do you know, Carla even had the gall to come here, to this house, when she heard he was back in London? Luckily he wasn't here. He'd gone off on that wild-goose chase to Devon, that time he hurt his hand, you know?"

Ivory shook her head. "He didn't tell me about that. He only said he tangled with some barbed wire."

"Typical! He nearly kills himself saving some stupid teenager, and then makes light of it. He'd heard a rumor that Andrea and Janey were in Devon, so he went down there to look for them. Some boys were messing about on a cliff and one of them slipped. He fell onto a ledge and Matthew climbed down to help him, sending the others to fetch help. It seems there was some barbed wire around—supposed to have been a fence but some vandal had wrecked it. Anyway, the boy was frightened and slipped again. He'd have fallen to his death if Matthew hadn't hung onto him. But he got his other hand caught in the barbed wire and couldn't let go or both of them would have fallen. Then the coast guard arrived and rescued them. But Matthew's hand was a mess. They said he was lucky not to have severed a nerve; as it was, he lost a lot of blood. And then only a few weeks later he got that blackmail note from Andrea, and soon after that there was the car accident. It was an awful time for him. Awful!''

Knowing that she had only made things worse for him, Ivory burst into tears she could no longer contain. Her stupid wish for revenge had ruined everything.

Nancy fussed round her, making her lie down, bringing a cold cloth to soothe her brow. "It's no good taking on so," she said worriedly. "You won't do yourself any good, or the baby."

Ivory opened her eyes, startled. "Baby?"

"Well, didn't you know? I could tell as soon as I saw you. You've got that peaked look some women have in the first few weeks. I expect you've been having morning sickness, haven't you?"

Closing her eyes tightly, Ivory reviewed the past few weeks. Yes, she had felt queasy some mornings, but she had put it down to worry. She couldn't be pregnant—unless it had happened that very first time, beside the fire in the cottage on the moors.

A baby! Matthew's baby, growing inside her. The thought made her feel fiercely protective, but it frightened her, too.

"You mustn't tell Matthew," she breathed. "Not yet. I don't want him to stay with me just because . . .''

Nancy resumed her seat, frowning. "It's really as bad as that, is it? Isn't he planning to take you to Australia with him?"

"He says not," Ivory croaked. "But he must give me a chance, Nancy. He must!"

When the phone rang, Nancy glanced at her watch and said, "That will be Harry, to tell me they're on their way. It usually takes about an hour. You lie there and relax, my dear. Everything's going to be fine."

She went out into the hall to answer the phone, and Ivory made herself relax, a hand over her eyes. In an hour's time she would know whether she was going to be given a chance of happiness, or whether her future would be a bleak void without Matthew, with only Janey—and the baby. The first Kendrake child to be born at the Hall; perhaps it would be a boy, a son for Matthew, born of a Meldrum. It might have seemed ironic, if it hadn't been so heartbreaking.

Sensing another presence, she looked round and saw Nancy in the doorway, her face a mask of tragedy. Ivory sat up, suddenly afraid.

"Now, you're not to worry!" Nancy said, hurrying to sit beside her. "But I'm afraid there's been an accident. They were on their way home. A child ran out into the road and Matthew ran to save him. But he's alive, Ivory. Hold on to that."

Chapter Twelve

Nancy drove her to the hospital. Ivory recalled greeting Harry Drummond, who told her more details of what had happened: the child had been saved, just had a bad fright. There were doctors and nurses, and there was Matthew, lying unconscious.

The head bandage looked shockingly white against his dark hair and skin, and his eyes were closed as if he would never open them again. He looked thinner than she remembered, with deep hollows under his cheekbones.

Looking at him, Ivory felt sick with fear.

That night she lay in bed at the Drummonds' house knowing she ought to sleep for the sake of the baby. But every time she closed her eyes she saw only Matthew, lying in the hospital bed with electrodes taped to his chest and a tube disappearing down his throat.

She was awakened by the sound of a phone. She threw on her dressing gown and rushed out to the stairs in time to hear Harry say, "Yes, I'll tell her. Thank you."

His face convinced Ivory that the news was not the worst, but he didn't look very happy. He came slowly up the stairs to take her hands. "He's conscious. The damage isn't as bad as they feared at first. There's no serious brain injury. Apart from that bump on his head, he's just got cuts and bruises. That's good news, isn't it?"

"Wonderful!" Ivory breathed, frightened by the "but" in his voice. "Then he'll be all right?"

"They think so. But—" His fingers tightened comfortingly on hers, though his eyes were troubled. "The problem is, Ivory, he can't remember a thing. He doesn't even know who he is."

Before she was allowed to see Matthew, Ivory had an interview with the doctor. He told her the amnesia was probably only a temporary thing, but advised her not to try to rush her husband's memory. He was to be kept in hospital for a while, until the head wound healed; that would give him time to adjust to the situation as far as was possible. After that, she could take him home.

Aware that she must stay calm for Matthew's sake, she followed a nurse to the private room where her husband lay. The nurse opened the door and said cheerfully, "Here's your wife to see you, Mr. Kendrake."

The bandage was still in place, but he looked better than he had the previous evening, almost his old self. But he had lost weight since he'd left Hedley Hall, and his blue eyes held an uncertain expression.

Knowing that to him she must seem like a stranger, Ivory said shyly, "Hello, Matthew. How are you feeling?"

"I'm fine," he said. "Apart from a headache. They've told you—"

"Yes. You don't remember anything. But that won't

last. Your memory will come back in its own good time, if you rest and get strong again. They've told me not to rush it."

"They told me the same, but, dammit, I don't even know your name!"

"It's Ivory."

"Ivory." He tested the sound as if he had never said it before. "Ivory." A frown drew his brows together. "I thought it would mean something, but it doesn't. I'm sorry."

"I understand. We'll take it very slowly." She drew a chair to the bedside and sat down, wanting to reach for his hand, wanting to weep, but knowing she mustn't. Why had he grown so thin? Had he been unhappy, as Nancy claimed?

"How long have we been married?" he asked.

"Two months."

"Is that all? Two months." He closed his eyes, leaning back against the pillows. "Good grief, we're still newlyweds, and I don't remember any of it."

Unable to hold back any longer, she took his hand between her own, entwining her fingers with his. "It's not important, darling. You will remember, in time. You're going to have to be patient, if you can manage it. Patience isn't one of your virtues."

He looked at her with the ghost of a wry smile, but his fingers tightened on hers as if the contact comforted him. "That's two things I know about myself."

"Two things?"

"I'm impatient, and I have very good taste when it comes to choosing a wife. I expect I've told you before, but . . . You're beautiful."

"Oh, Matthew!" Ready tears rushed into her eyes, and she bent her head to hide them.

"Hey, now," he said softly, touching her hair with a tentative hand. "Don't go to pieces on me. I'm going to need your strength. We'll see this through together, won't we?" An anxious note had crept into his voice, and Ivory lifted her head to see the doubts and bewilderment in those forget-me-not eyes. "You will stay with me, won't you?"

"Of course I will," she breathed. "I've got no life without you. I love you, Matthew."

Frowning a little, he rubbed her cheek with the back of his hand. "Two months. Good Lord! Imagine forgetting the happiest time of my life!"

It was going to be even more difficult than she had supposed.

She informed Mrs. Barnes of what had happened, but told her not to alarm Janey. While Matthew remained in hospital, she stayed with the Drummonds and visited her husband twice daily, telling him very little. The doctors had said that by going into detail she would only irritate him, since it would seem like a story about someone else. Until he remembered for himself, until he remembered his own attitudes and feelings, there was no point in recounting his life history. So she told him only that she was his second wife and that he had a daughter from his first marriage.

Some days Matthew was irritable, angry with himself and angry with everyone around him; then he would be sorry. He had every reason to believe that the condition was only temporary, but it frustrated him. Matthew Kendrake did not like to feel helpless, as Ivory well knew. If it was difficult for her, it was worse for him.

After a few days the bandage was replaced by a plaster, and she could see they had shaved part of his hair. But it would grow again, and the unruly tumble around it partially concealed the place. To outward appearances, he was almost back to normal.

The Drummonds proved themselves true friends.

Harry even drove Ivory's car back to Hedley Magna, since the Mercedes was available for her in London. He returned by train and reported that Janey was well, but anxious to see her father and Ivory. Ivory phoned the child every day.

After two weeks she was able to tell Janey that they were coming home and would all go on holiday together. After long talks with the doctor, and encouraged by Nancy, she had decided to take Matthew to the cottage on the moors, where they could live a quiet family life away from inquisitive neighbors.

When, finally, she drove north with Matthew beside her, the yellow of autumn was beginning to shade the trees. Matthew had regained some weight while in hospital. For a different reason, her own waistline had thickened, but as yet only she was aware of it.

Seeing him frowning at road signs, she said quietly, "Don't try to force it, Matthew. They told you at the hospital—"

"I know what they told me!" he cut in, and sighed, laying an intimate hand on her knee. "I'm sorry, darling, but I keep looking for something that will turn the key. If you only knew what it's like to be in a mental no-man's-land."

"I can imagine," she replied, wondering if he would ever regret calling her "darling." She used the endearment naturally, but he said it only to follow suit. In some ways, as she had told herself many times, she was deceiving him yet again by pretending they were happily married. Except that it wasn't pretence. Between them now there was a warmth and understanding that she had never dared hope for. But would it last after he remembered what had gone before?

She was afraid that Hedley Hall might provide the key he was seeking. Or perhaps Janey would stir his memory. She knew it was selfish of her to be afraid.

She wanted Matthew to be well again. But what if it meant their parting? As the miles sped by beneath the wheels she grew more and more tense, waiting for some familiar landmark to open the door for him.

For her a lifetime of memories lay in the sight of Hedley Magna with its red roofs among the trees, the lane where the cottage stood with smoke marks still smudged across its walls, and then Hedley Hall, glowing golden in the autumn sunlight. But when she glanced at Matthew, she could see it meant nothing to him.

"Here's Janey," she told him as the little girl appeared on the porch with Mrs. Barnes, beside the wooden tub filled with bronze chrysanthemums.

As Matthew stepped out of the car, Janey ran out onto the gravel but paused uncertainly, having been told her father was not well. Matthew, however, was equal to the occasion. He said, "Hello, Janey," and held out his arms.

"Oh, Daddy! Daddy!" Janey rushed at him, clinging tightly round his neck as he lifted her off the ground.

"Don't strain yourself, Matthew," Ivory said worriedly.

"I won't," he said in an odd, taut voice, bending his face to Janey's curls. Ivory saw the glint of moisture on his lashes and was moved to tears herself. She knew why he was upset: not even the sight of his daughter had jogged his closed memory.

She tried to keep everything as normal as possible. While Matthew rested, she put Janey to bed and then called him to say good night, leaving the two of them alone. She poured him an aperitif and, they dined by candlelight on the steak Diane Mrs. Barnes had prepared especially.

Later they sat in the drawing room, finishing the wine that had accompanied the meal. Ivory drank very little of it, because of the baby, but she kept refilling Matthew's glass. As the alcohol took its effect, she saw him relax. He began to talk more freely, recalling incidents that had occurred at the hospital with a dry humor which made her laugh.

"I must be a very lucky man," he said eventually, gazing at her with the strange, half-despairing look that had become familiar to her. "This house, good friends, a pretty daughter, and you, Ivory. You know why I'm sitting here making conversation, don't you?"

"Because you feel like a visitor?" she suggested.

He shook his head, smiling wryly. "Because I want to take you to bed. And since I hardly know you, it feels vaguely immoral."

"There's nothing immoral about it," she assured him softly. "I'm your wife. Give me ten minutes, will you?"

"Is that what I did the first time?"

Flushing, Ivory laughed a little guiltily. "Not exactly. But then, this is almost like the first time, isn't it? For you, anyway."

"Suppose I've forgotten how to do that, too?" he asked with another twisted smile.

"If you have," she said, bending to kiss him lightly, "I'll remind you."

She waited in the bedroom, clad in a white lace negligee she had bought for just this occasion, because he had once said she ought to wear virginal white. Nerves made her laugh at the thought: a virgin bride with a baby forming in her womb.

She heard him in the dressing room. Eventually he came in wearing the brown silk robe she had laid out for him. He looked as diffident as a boy with his first girl. But his body beneath the robe was all mature man, making her heart begin to thump erratically.

As she stood up, he drew a long, deep breath, and his

glance devoured her from head to foot. Desire gleamed
in his bright blue eyes. But there was tenderness, too,
such as she had never seen in him before. This is the
real Matthew, she thought, without his defences, without that barrier round his heart.

"I love you," she whispered, holding out her arms.

Two jerky strides brought him to her side, and he
clasped her in his arms, seeking her willing lips. After
weeks of brief pecks exchanged in hospital, this first
real embrace shook her with its intensity and made her
as impatient as he. Only minutes later they lay naked
on the bed, lost in each other.

Afterwards, Matthew lay with his head on her breast,
one hand playing with her hair and touching her face.
He lifted himself to look at her in the dim light, a gentle
finger wiping the tears from her cheek.

"Why are you crying?"

"Because I love you so much," she breathed. "You'll
never know how much I love you."

"I think I do," he said, and began to kiss her again.
"You're so lovely, little wife of mine. Like an ivory
statue. Only softer, and warmer. I feel like a bride-
groom. Is this how it was? I'm lucky to be able to
experience it twice. Ivory, darling Ivory."

She gave herself to the joy of being loved. It was a
guilty joy, though, because she was stealing it from
him. When he knew she had deceived him about their
relationship, would he hate her even more than he had
hated her before his accident?

The following day, they drove farther north toward
the Yorkshire moors, with Janey in the back seat
talking excitedly about the coming holiday. Once more
Ivory was prey to a flood of alternating hopes and fears
as she followed the same route Matthew had used on

their honeymoon journey. But this time he seemed content just to watch the scenery of soft greens counterpointed with scarlet and tan in the trees. Occasionally he laid his hand on her thigh, squeezing gently, and she glanced round to exchange a smile with him. They were almost reliving their honeymoon, the way it should have been the first time, without the animosity that had dogged their original journey.

They reached the cottage by mid-afternoon. Ivory had asked Mrs. Wheeler to prepare for their arrival but not to bother baking; she herself intended to do all the cooking, to provide a real family life for Matthew and Janey.

"Oh, it's lovely!" Janey exclaimed, rushing around to look at everything. "Which is my room? Can I go upstairs?"

She scampered away, while Matthew stood in the middle of the kitchen taking a low, slow look all around him. Ivory watched, her heart thudding.

At last he looked at her, trying to conceal his disappointment. "What's this place called?"

"I'm not sure. You christened it Honeymoon Cottage the first time we came."

His smile was bleak. "Appropriate, I suppose. Now we're here on a second honeymoon. For a moment I thought—something about the smell of the place. But it's gone, whatever it was."

"You must let it take its own time," she said.

"I know, but it's so damnably . . . Sometimes I think I'm on the verge of remembering, then it's as if the curtain falls again. Like being lost in impenetrable fog. I even wonder if I really want to remember. The doctor did say that amnesia sometimes happens because the patient has been through some trauma that he wants to forget. Is that how it was with me? Did that bump on the head give me an opportunity that I grabbed to slip into limbo?"

Ivory ran to him, clasping her arms around him to hold him tightly. "Whatever it was, it doesn't matter. We'll be quiet here. Just you and me and Janey. You can go walking, and sketching, if you like. I've brought the materials."

"Sketching?" He reached into the back pocket of his slacks and took out his wallet, opening it to extract a sheet of folded paper. It was his sketch of her. "Did I do this myself?"

"Yes, apparently you did." Her hand trembled as she took the paper from him, seeing the simple line drawing that managed to make her look beautiful. "It's flattering."

"If it is, it's probably because I looked at you with the eyes of a lover. Personally, I don't think it does you justice."

She refolded the paper, keeping her head bent. If he knew she was crying again he would wonder why, and she just might have to tell him. She escaped on the pretext of looking for Janey.

Days filled with autumn color followed. On the moor the heather was dying, turning dark brown. The bracken beside the stream glowed orange, and the sycamores dripped golden leaves that shimmered in the sunlight.

Now and then Matthew's impatience came to the surface, but mostly he was careful to hide it. Ivory was aware of it simmering beneath the apparent calm. If he had just accepted his condition, he wouldn't have been Matthew. Nevertheless, she was surprised by his forbearance. But the slow, simple life of the cottage seemed to soothe him, and at night he found respite in her arms. Whatever the future held, she knew she would never regret those nights—or those days when she was simply his wife and Janey's mother.

One evening, as she washed the dishes after seeing Janey safely to bed, Matthew came in looking for a screwdriver to fix a wobbly hinge on the sitting room door.

"I think there are some tools in that far drawer," Ivory said.

She heard him rooting in the drawer, then there was a silence that made her glance round. Her heart almost stopped as she saw what he had in his hand: the jewelry box she had thrown into that drawer after he left her alone at the cottage. Hardly daring to breathe, she watched as he opened the box and looked at the pendant inside it.

"That's a strange place to keep jewelry," he said slowly. "Is it yours?"

"Yes."

Her voice was so faint that he looked up sharply and saw how pale she had grown. "Why is it in a tool drawer?"

"I threw it in there. I was angry. I'd forgotten all about it until—"

For a split second she fancied she saw the blue demon glare at her, then it was gone and Matthew said, "Why were you angry?"

"Because—because you had been called away on business. In the middle of our honeymoon. That pendant seemed like an easy way of placating me. I wasn't thinking straight. I just hurled it into the first drawer that came to hand and—and forgot about it."

Very slowly, he picked the pendant out of its box, letting it dangle from its chain. He walked across the kitchen and fastened the emerald round her neck, his fingers caressing her skin. Cupping her face in both hands, he looked somberly down into her eyes. "Am I such an ogre?"

"No!" She flung her arms round his neck and clung

to him, her face against his throat. "Sometimes there's a devil that gets into you, that's all. But I'm not perfect myself. I love you just the way you are."

"I love you, too," he said, his arms tightening around her. "I'll just fix that hinge and . . . Shall we have an early night?"

Ivory concurred, but her happiness was spoiled, as it always was, by the guilt that grew worse with every day that passed. He said he loved her, but she didn't know if it was true. He used the phrase as a convention, when what he meant was that he wanted her—as he had once made her say to him. Matthew in his right senses scorned the word love. He had made that very clear. And if he didn't soon remember, she would have to tell him. This false happiness was tearing her apart.

The following morning, while she helped Janey with sums, Matthew went out with his sketchbook. Ivory was so absorbed in watching the way her stepdaughter's mind was expanding that she failed to notice the weather until the light in the kitchen grew so gloomy she almost needed to switch on a light. Alarmed, she saw mist floating across the windows. It had crept up suddenly, as it could do on the moors.

"Stay here, Janey," she said hurriedly. "I'm just going out to see if I can see Daddy coming. It's nearly time for lunch."

Throwing on an anorak, she went out into the creeping grayness that cloaked the valley. She began to walk to where the track petered out in short grass, but paused and looked back as the sound of an engine reached her. A car came slowly up the track and stopped a few yards from where she stood transfixed with dismay. It was a low red sports car.

"Well, this really is the back of beyond, isn't it?" Carla Forsythe said, strolling toward Ivory with a smile that had no warmth in it.

"What are you doing here?" Ivory demanded, her throat suddenly thick with apprehension. Carla could ruin everything.

"I came to see Matthew, of course," the redhead said. She wore a pink track suit with very tight pants and a blouse fastened by tiestrings at waist and neck, the hood thrown back to reveal her bright hair. "Though I must say, you've hidden him away pretty well. Even knowing the address I've had a terrible time finding this place."

"Who gave you the address?" Ivory managed.

Carla looked her up and down, her green eyes glittering with malice. "Your gullible Mrs. Barnes, of course. I told her I wanted to send a get-well card, but I was coming up here for a break, anyway—I've got friends in Scarborough—so I thought I'd bring my good wishes in person. Where is he?"

"Out. Out walking."

"In this weather?" The green eyes grew round with amazement. "My dear girl, is he fit enough to be traipsing around the moors in a fog? Alone?"

"He's perfectly fit." Ivory was trembling, her hands clenched so tightly that her nails bit into her palms. "Carla, you'll have to leave. You can't see him yet. There isn't any point. He won't know you."

"I'm aware of that. But hasn't it occurred to you that the sight of me might jog his memory? I've known him for a very long time, you know. Or does it suit you better to have him totally under your control? Isn't that why you took him away from Hedley Hall?"

"No, it isn't. Please, Carla. Please go away. You'll only upset him."

The redhead's eyes narrowed, then flicked beyond Ivory's pale face. Her malicious smile reappeared. "Too late, I'm afraid. Here he comes now."

She set off up the track, where Matthew's tall figure

was visible as he came slowly down from the moor. He had had the foresight to take a sheepskin jacket with him, for which Ivory was thankful. But her head seemed about to burst with the terror of what Carla's arrival might do. She herself began to walk up the track, knowing that nothing could stop Carla from creating whatever mischief she had planned.

"Darling, hello!" Carla called as she came within hailing distance of Matthew. "Your wife's furious with me, but I told her you wouldn't mind a visit from an old friend."

"Old friend?" Matthew's voice came to Ivory. His eyes sought her and he walked past Carla, who turned to trot beside him.

"I'm Carla," she told him. "Carla Forsythe. Don't you remember?"

"No, I'm afraid I don't," Matthew said, making straight for Ivory. He slipped an arm round her shoulders and bent to kiss her tenderly. "Hello, darling. Sorry I've been so long. Were you worried?"

"Yes, a little bit," she confessed, hugging him. "You're cold."

"I'm fine," he said, smiling down at her.

Carla's mouth had pinched into a moue of spitefulness. "This is a tender scene, Matthew, but you ought to know your wife isn't the perfect little helpmeet she appears to be. I don't doubt she's been putting up a good show, but has she told you she only married you for your money? She came as your daughter's nanny, and got her greedy little hooks into you within a few weeks. When you found out what she was really like, you left her."

Held in the grip of an awful panic, Ivory stared up at her husband's face, her arms locked round his waist as if she could protect him from Carla's words. She saw him frown with puzzlement.

"Did you say you were an old friend?" he asked Carla.

"Of very long standing," she replied meaningfully. "In fact, if this little golddigger hadn't come along, I'd probably be your wife by now."

Matthew's frown deepened, but his voice was calm enough. "Then all I can say is, thank God Ivory saved me from that fate. You've been here five minutes, and in that short time you've tried to wreck my marriage and put doubts into a mind that's confused enough already. You're no friend of mine, Miss . . . whatever your name is."

"My God!" Carla got out. "She's really conned you, hasn't she? Well, when you do finally come to your senses, don't come running to me for consolation. I've had it with you, Matthew Kendrake." She glared at Ivory, who was nestled close in her husband's arms. "I wish you joy of each other," was her parting jibe as she swung away to stride back to her car.

Ivory rubbed her face on the soft lapel of Matthew's coat, her eyes filling with tears. "Oh, Matthew!" she said brokenly. "I hope you won't ever regret that. In a way, she's right. I haven't been entirely honest with—"

His hand lifted her chin and his lips prevented the confession she had been about to make. She let herself enjoy his embrace one last bittersweet time before she told him the truth. She had to tell him now, whatever came of it.

But it seemed that he didn't want her to speak. One hand held her head in a viselike grip and his other arm was so tight about her she could hardly breathe. His mouth had become savage; his body was rigid against hers. The despair she sensed in him frightened her.

When he lifted his head, she stared at him through a film of tears, and opened her mouth to say something. It died in her throat as she saw the expression on his face. The bitter lines about his lips; the glinting blue eyes—they belonged to a Matthew who remembered all that lay between them, a Matthew whose devil had come back.

She eased herself away from him, her heart pounding in her throat. "Matthew? You remember?"

"Everything," he said hoarsely, turning his shoulder to her as he thrust his hands deep into the pockets of his sheepskin and stared at the mist. "When I saw the clouds coming . . . I remembered looking for you that time. The rest followed as though someone had turned a switch. Good God"— he dashed a hand through his hair distractedly—"why didn't you *tell* me?"

Hopelessly, she slumped inside her jacket. The mist seemed twice as cold, swirling round them as if they were trapped in some netherworld of grayness. "There didn't seem to be any point. I didn't want to deceive you, but they told me to let you remember in your own good time. I can't apologize for it. I know I've stolen these last few days from you, but—"

"*You* have?" He whirled on her, his face contorted with anguish. "*I'm* the one who's been taking everything. After the way I treated you, you ought to have left me to stew!"

"Matthew, no!"

"Yes! Don't be kind any longer, for God's sake. I remember the way I behaved. I don't deserve what you've done for me, Ivory. I'm grateful, but— Dear heaven, is there any wonder I blanked it all out?" He walked to the stone wall that surrounded the cottage and sat down there, his head in his hands.

"But it was my own fault," she said, following him. "Please, Matthew, I'm not being kind, I'm being honest. My motives for coming back to the Hall *were* muddled. I admit that. I had a crazy idea I could even the score. But that isn't why I married you. I realized it wasn't important anymore, even before I found out the truth."

His head came up and he looked at her dazedly, as if he didn't follow what she was saying. "What truth?"

"About your uncle. Old Mrs. Mead told me. I know the whole village has misjudged your uncle all these years because he was too much of a gentleman—maybe too loving—to come out in public and call my grandmother a liar. But she did it because she loved my grandfather. I can't blame her for that."

"For heaven's sake, all that was ages ago. It doesn't matter."

"But it does!" she insisted. "It made you hate me. I realize now I ought to have thought of talking to Mrs. Mead before I ever came to the Hall, but it never occurred to me. Besides, if I'd done that we—we might never have met."

"You make it sound as though that would have been a tragedy," he said bitterly.

Her eyes filled with warm tears as she muttered, "It would have been, for me."

"Ivory." He reached out and caught her hands, pulling her closer to him, his face lifted to hers. "How can you say that? I punished you with all the bitterness I felt for Andrea. I made myself believe you were like her. But Andrea wouldn't have stuck with me the way you've done, putting up with my moods this past month—and before, when there was less excuse. I know how I must have hurt you. Don't you want to be free of me?"

She shook her head, choking, "It was *you* who was going to leave *me*."

"I was out of my mind," he said.

Sobbing, she threw her arms round his neck and held him tightly, feeling his arms close round her. She rubbed her face against his mist-damp hair. And as he lifted his head, she bent to kiss his mouth feverishly, her tears wetting his face.

He pulled her onto his lap, cradling her as if she were a child, wrapping her securely with his arms and his body while he kissed the tears from her eyes, his lips hard and warm against her skin. "Ivory, Ivory, Ivory," he murmured. "You must take after your grandmother."

"How do you mean?" she asked, blinking in bewilderment.

"You've done what you've done," he said in a low voice, "because you love your husband."

Her sight blurred through a fresh scald of tears. "Yes, I have. If only you would believe me!"

"I do believe you," he muttered against her mouth. "Darling love, you've proved it a dozen times over."

Joy surged through her as she gave herself up to his kisses, returning them with equal passion until her head was spinning and her blood singing through her veins.

"And I love you," he said hoarsely. "Love you, want you, need you. Darling Ivory, don't you know that? Hasn't it been obvious to you?"

She buried her face in the warmth of his throat, her lips touching the pulse that beat beneath his skin. She wondered why she was still crying when she was so happy.

"Ever since we met I've been fighting a battle with my own feelings," he told her gruffly. "I was so jealous of Rob Garth I could have killed him. When he told me about your grandparents, it seemed to confirm all my worst suspicions. I think I must have gone slightly mad. Forgive me."

"There's nothing to forgive," she whispered. "If you love me, nothing else matters."

"Then will you do something for me?" he breathed in her ear.

"Anything!"

A finger beneath her chin made her look at him, and she saw his eyes gleam with rueful amusement. "Will you please get up? My leg's going to sleep."

Biting her lip against a bubble of giddy laughter, Ivory pushed herself unsteadily to her feet, not caring that her hair was tousled and her face tear-streaked. "Sorry."

"Don't apologize. I ought to have chosen somewhere more comfortable." Holding her hand, he eased himself off the wall and stamped his foot to get the blood flowing again.

"Matthew," she said thoughtfully. "When Carla was here just now, you did know who she was. You deliberately sent her packing."

His eyebrow quirked, no longer maddening, but endearing. "Yes, I did. It seemed the simplest way of dealing with her. Damn the woman, I'm sick of having her chasing after me."

"Then—I'm sorry, but I've got to know. Why did you go to her that night after you found out I was a Meldrum?"

A heavy sigh escaped him as he grimaced. "I didn't, actually. I called her, in a fit of pique, but I didn't meet her. When it came to it, she was the last person I wanted to see. It would have been cheap revenge, with a woman I can't stand. I went drinking, and came in very late, so I slept in the dressing room. Believe me?"

"Yes, and I'm glad. I was so jealous you wouldn't believe it."

"Wouldn't I?" Head on one side, he smiled wryly at her. "While we're on the subject of third parties: had you arranged to meet Rob Garth in Holly Wood that day you went to see old Mrs. Mead?"

"How can you ask that?" she demanded, wounded afresh. "Of course I didn't arrange it. We ran into each other, that's all. Oh, I knew that must be what sent you off in such a tearing hurry!"

"I saw him kissing you," he informed her.

"He wasn't kissing me! Just a brush on the cheek. A last good-bye, because he knew I was in love with you. Rob was never any more than a friend. It was completely innocent—not like your relationship with Carla Forsythe."

"What relationship? A few kisses in the heat of the moment is all it ever was with Carla."

"But there were others?" She was riven with jealousy, and the leap of laughter in his eyes only incensed her more.

"A few," he said, lips twitching. "Brief physical liaisons, with no strings on either side. I'm not going to apologize for that, since it happened before I knew you. Have I asked about your private life?"

"It wouldn't matter if you had. There's nothing to tell."

"Nothing at all? Not even some passionate clinches? If so, there must have been something wrong with the male students at your college."

"Matthew, it's not funny!" she cried.

"No." He reached for her, drawing her into his arms and holding her tightly against him, the demon glaring covetously at her. "No, it's deadly serious. If some other man had made love to you before me, I'd probably find him and kill him."

He kissed her with a possessive passion that made her heart leap. She had the real Matthew back. His old devilish self, mixed with the gentler man she had known for the past month.

"Let's go in and take these coats off," he said eventually, breathing unevenly. "Can you find Janey something absorbing to do for an hour—or two?"

"Not when there isn't a lock on the bedroom door,"

she said, laughing. "Besides, she'll be wanting her lunch. You'll just have to be patient."

"Which, as you reminded me, is not one of my virtues. I'm not the easiest of men to live with, I suppose. I won't change, you know. An arrogant brute. Isn't that what you called me?"

"Your memory's back with a vengeance," she said ruefully. "Yes, you can be difficult, but these last few days . . . It's been heaven, Matthew, except that you weren't well and I was afraid what you'd say when—"

He stopped the words with another kiss, a wicked, lingering kiss that made her knees go weak. "It's been heaven for me, too," he said, his voice deep and tender. "For the first time in my life I've discovered what it can feel like to love someone who really loves me in return."

Clasping her arms round his neck, she rubbed her face against his. "And this is the man who said he was incapable of love."

"Ah, well," he sighed, "I had to protect myself somehow. But it was self-delusion. Good grief, after I'd written that letter I was so wretched. No wonder I wiped it all out. I couldn't live with it."

"So you won't leave me."

His arms hardened round her. "Never. What's mine I keep, remember? And to prove it—You know what I'd really like to do?"

"No, what?"

"Get married again, properly, in church. Have our union blessed, or whatever they call it. Invite all the tenants from the estate. What do you think?"

"It's a wonderful idea!" she breathed. "We'll make them see the Kendrakes in a different light. And if I buy you a wedding ring, will you wear it?"

"With pride," he assured her.

Filled with a warm sense of rightness, she reached up

to kiss him softly. "The only thing is, darling, we shall have to arrange it soon or I'll never fit into a wedding dress. Though I suppose that in this case it won't be too shocking that the bride is pregnant."

He stared down at her incredulously. "What?"

"I'm afraid so," she said, happily snuggling against him. "It must have happened that very first time—after I got lost in the mist, remember? Mist must be lucky for us. Are you pleased?"

"Pleased?" he murmured vibrantly in her ear. "I could jump over the moon! A brother for Janey. Our son. It's got to be a boy."

She wrinkled her nose at him, seeing that the demon hadn't disappeared. It was dancing with delight. It was part of him, and she wouldn't have it any other way. "If you order it to be a boy, it hasn't got much choice, has it?" she teased. "Though if it takes after its father, it will be whatever it pleases."

"Witch!" he retorted, laughing, and bent to sweep her off the ground, into his arms, beginning to carry her with slow, steady steps toward the cottage. "Right, Mrs. Kendrake. This is where *I* start taking care of *you* for a change."

Silhouette Romance

IT'S YOUR OWN SPECIAL TIME

Contemporary romances for today's women.
Each month, six very special love stories will be yours
from SILHOUETTE. Look for them wherever books are sold
or order now from the coupon below.

$1.50 each

☐ 5 Goforth	☐ 28 Hampson	☐ 54 Beckman	☐ 83 Halston
☐ 6 Stanford	☐ 29 Wildman	☐ 55 LaDame	☐ 84 Vitek
☐ 7 Lewis	☐ 30 Dixon	☐ 56 Trent	☐ 85 John
☐ 8 Beckman	☐ 32 Michaels	☐ 57 John	☐ 86 Adams
☐ 9 Wilson	☐ 33 Vitek	☐ 58 Stanford	☐ 87 Michaels
☐ 10 Caine	☐ 34 John	☐ 59 Vernon	☐ 88 Stanford
☐ 11 Vernon	☐ 35 Stanford	☐ 60 Hill	☐ 89 James
☐ 17 John	☐ 38 Browning	☐ 61 Michaels	☐ 90 Major
☐ 19 Thornton	☐ 39 Sinclair	☐ 62 Halston	☐ 92 McKay
☐ 20 Fulford	☐ 46 Stanford	☐ 63 Brent	☐ 93 Browning
☐ 22 Stephens	☐ 47 Vitek	☐ 71 Ripy	☐ 94 Hampson
☐ 23 Edwards	☐ 48 Wildman	☐ 73 Browning	☐ 95 Wisdom
☐ 24 Healy	☐ 49 Wisdom	☐ 76 Hardy	☐ 96 Beckman
☐ 25 Stanford	☐ 50 Scott	☐ 78 Oliver	☐ 97 Clay
☐ 26 Hastings	☐ 52 Hampson	☐ 81 Roberts	☐ 98 St. George
☐ 27 Hampson	☐ 53 Browning	☐ 82 Dailey	☐ 99 Camp

$1.75 each

☐ 100 Stanford	☐ 110 Trent	☐ 120 Carroll	☐ 130 Hardy
☐ 101 Hardy	☐ 111 South	☐ 121 Langan	☐ 131 Stanford
☐ 102 Hastings	☐ 112 Stanford	☐ 122 Scofield	☐ 132 Wisdom
☐ 103 Cork	☐ 113 Browning	☐ 123 Sinclair	☐ 133 Rowe
☐ 104 Vitek	☐ 114 Michaels	☐ 124 Beckman	☐ 134 Charles
☐ 105 Eden	☐ 115 John	☐ 125 Bright	☐ 135 Logan
☐ 106 Dailey	☐ 116 Lindley	☐ 126 St. George	☐ 136 Hampson
☐ 107 Bright	☐ 117 Scott	☐ 127 Roberts	☐ 137 Hunter
☐ 108 Hampson	☐ 118 Dailey	☐ 128 Hampson	☐ 138 Wilson
☐ 109 Vernon	☐ 119 Hampson	☐ 129 Converse	☐ 139 Vitek

Genuine Silhouette
sterling silver bookmark
for only $15.95!

What a beautiful way to hold your place in your current romance! This genuine sterling silver bookmark, with the distinctive Silhouette symbol in elegant black, measures 1½" long and 1" wide. It makes a beautiful gift for yourself, and for every romantic you know! And, at only $15.95 each, including all postage and handling charges, you'll want to order several now, while supplies last.

Send your name and address with check or money order for $15.95 per bookmark ordered to
Simon & Schuster Enterprises
120 Brighton Rd., P.O. Box 5020
Clifton, N.J. 07012
Attn: Bookmark

Bookmarks can be ordered pre-paid only. No charges will be accepted. Please allow 4-6 weeks for delivery.

N.Y. State Residents
Please Add Sales Tax